THE
KNOCK

"Look," said Cowley, his voice turning serious. There was a strange almost fanatical gleam in his bright blue eyes. "There is a production line in tabloid newspapers, we all know it. It starts with the small town papers and works its way through the bigger city papers covering the larger industrial areas and ends up in Fleet Street and what's the common thread? The common thread is knocking on doors. It's where all the big stories are made, on the doorstep. Our kind of paper is a halfway house between the small and the huge. We are messengers swooping on every bit of misfortune we see on the screen, fax or in the classified columns, notably deaths. We are the link between the small and the big, we find the stories that grow like snowballs until they make the nationals."

THE KNOCK

PETER TAYLOR

Library of Congress Control Number: 2014902178
ISBN: Hardcover   978-1-4931-4087-9
                 Softcover   978-1-4931-4085-5
                 eBook   978-1-4931-4086-2

Rev. date: 04/04/2014

To order additional copies of this book, contact:
Xlibris LLC
0-800-056-3182
www.xlibrispublishing.co.uk
Orders@xlibrispublishing.co.uk
522259

One

SIX a.m. The phone snapped him awake in the darkness of his bedroom. The voice of Holmes, his news editor boss, chiselled at his head. "Can you get in here quick? I'm a man down and it's all kicking off." That was all, a mouthful of words and Holmes was gone. No hello, no goodbye. No inquiries in to how he was today. He threw the quilt to one side and got up. He shaved quickly but carefully in the half light of the bathroom. The chipped tiles, faulty shower and mouldy ceiling did little to lighten his mood. Its small window was covered in light rain. A cold, grey northern England day ruled the streets outside and he was reluctant to embrace its welcome. He was low man on the totem pole alright, someone who could be kicked out of bed two hours earlier than the time set down there in black and white in his work contract.

He ran a hand through his thick, tufty brown hair and tugged his curly sideboards, pulling and shaking himself awake. He looked at himself in the small hand mirror he was using to shave. The same old feeling that something was not right. The same old voice in his head. "George, what on earth are you doing with your life?" His questioning inner self on the rampage again. All it needed was a hint of daylight and it was out of the box and haring for the murky woodlands of his mind in search of its prey, down the foxholes of doubt, insecurity, uncertainty, fear, confusion and vulnerability, just like a Beagle hunting rabbits. And, just like a Beagle, it nearly always got its teeth in to something.

"What's a quiet village boy from the chalky downs of Sussex doing up here in the north, mortgaged to a pokey den and a clapped-out car, in Gateshead, England, where men are men and rain is forever and why? Where are you going? What are you doing?"

He knew the answer, of course, but he kept it to himself. It was no good, in the 21st century, to go around telling people you wanted to be a writer. They were of the past, haunting voices of history. His own feeling was that the 21st century was not a place with much time for scribblers, dreamers, people who wanted to use words to achieve something of beauty or meaning.

"You're in the wrong time and the wrong place," his voice would tell him. "And you have no answer. Do you?"

He had found no answer in newspaper journalism. That was true. It had been a false trail leading him well astray. His fellow travellers on this path were mostly hard-faced, hard-nosed diggers of facts, ready to fight each other as well as anybody else to complete their tasks, and pressurised to the hilt. There was no time to write, only time to report.

They were rushed from one assignment to another until the day's printing ended. There was no time to reach for words of import, phrases of enlightenment, the poetry of syntax and composition.

He found a white shirt in the standing wardrobe which, along with the bedside table unit, formed the bedroom's two items of furniture. A small beer fridge, always full, also doubled as a stand for his television, a 28-inch plasma which was the most modern item in his flat. The shirt was followed by a black well-worn pinstripe suit and black shoes. He threw a thick coat on and made his way down the three floors which led from his flat to the street outside where his old Ford seemed as miserable as him and would only start on the third attempt.

His headlights picked out concrete buildings in the darkness, the river and then all the steel around it. He put Yellow by Coldplay on his car audio player and turned up the volume. A driving wall of electric guitar sound was the perfect answer to the colourless pre-dawn. He motored on in his warm metal bubble, singing loudly to lift his spirits.

This side of the city provided its most imposing view, all bridges and buildings, no greenery, just concrete and steel, the essence of the business powerhouse of Newcastle-upon-Tyne. Robert Stephenson's High Level Bridge had girdered its way in to history in 1849 brutally splitting the castle which gave the city its name in to isolated sections. Around it on the skyline was an awesome mix of history: church and cathedral spires; the gaudy football stadium; elegant Georgian buildings which banked down to the quayside; the castle keep; the medieval walls; the railway. He stared for the umpteenth time at the huge billboard which dwarfed the city's smart quayside from the gable end of a block of plush flats overlooking the Tyne. It said:

THE METROPOLIS

News am to pm every day

His employer. The new kid on the block in the ever diminishing world of print newspapers in the city that was once England's coalhouse. The Metropolis had been as welcome as a fox in a chicken run when it opened its doors for business just one year ago. The consortium behind it had spotted a gap in the market and moved in almost overnight.

The gap was this. Newcastle had been served for the best part of two centuries by national newspapers which brought yesterday's news and proud regional morning to evening newspapers which updated them by bringing all the significant news of the day, both local and national.

The nationals still did much the same job but the internet and the great recession had changed things for the Courier and the Sentinel, regionals which had ruled the roost in the city for 200 years and more. Readers were deserting their printed pages in their thousands and the corporate bosses, instead of devising new ways to attract them, took the hump.

They were ostriches, heads buried in the swirling sands of real estate and newsprint costs. They cut staff and the easiest staff to cut were the hacks who brought the news. They stopped running hourly editions. The papers were mostly made up the day before and all the old deadlines were scrapped—no more news updates at 12 noon, 1pm, 2pm and then late night final deadlines. They stopped printing on Sundays. They even considered printing just twice a week.

The old guard were mesmerized by the internet and the pull it had on young people who should be reading their newspapers. They started investing heavily in the technology to bring professional online news services while heaping more work on fewer journalists expected to produce printed and online news. A reporter whose main worry before had been to get the contents of his notebook over the phone to his editor was now expected to capture videos and pictures with his smartphone. Pictures, pictures, pictures was the mantra of the industry. Faces, talking heads, family photos. Every picture told a story. Every story had to have a picture.

A reporter was expected to think pictures just as much as words. He was to be a multimedia journalist, a job title which basically meant many more responsibilities for the same pay.

There were a whole host of other things expected of newsprint industry trained men and women which cheesed them off. The new buzzword was flexibility and it meant: "Just do everything you're told or you are expendable."

There was so much competition to get in to the supposedly glamorous world of journalism that hacks were ten a penny. Their services were cheap. The Metropolis saw its chance and strode in to town with its am to pm service.

The consortium behind it leased some prestige top floors in Grey Street in the historic centre of the city for its editorial and advertising staff and set up an out-of-town printing and distribution depot. The consortium was a mystery which the financial press was still trying to pin down. It was known that a Venezuelan multi-millionaire had wanted to offload a lot of money in to a safe haven out of fear of becoming a kidnap target in his own country. Crime in Venezuela was massive and rich, powerful people lived in fear of kidnap for ransom by ruthless crime gangs. The multi-millionaire had a fleet of helicopters and limousines and a small army of bodyguards but he feared his family was vulnerable. The gangs would kidnap any member of it to hold for ransom, even his small children or his nephews and nieces. His fear of this was so great he went to inconceivable lengths to disguise his identity. The faceless VZOL consortium was set up with the help of advisors and it had spent some time unsuccessfully trying to buy a football club in England before it fell under the spell of one, Robert Morton, an ex-Fleet Street editor who refused to believe, as everyone else in the industry did, that the regional newspaper industry was in terminal decline. It was Morton, the newsprint mastermind, who was behind the sudden arrival of The Metropolis in Newcastle and several other cities across the United Kingdom and Ireland. The money poured in from South America.

Lots of the news reporters sacked in Newcastle by the old guard as it downsized operations were taken on by The Metropolis. One of them was George Sharpe, a 27-year-old business studies graduate, who had spent two years travelling the world, after his studies in Leicestershire, England, before deciding the last thing he wanted to do was be a businessman. He then made what he now considered to be one of his biggest mistakes by deciding to work for one year as a reporter on a tired old evening newspaper in a town ten miles east of where he worked now.

Sharpe parked his car at a spot on the quayside where he could leave it for free all day. He now faced an uphill walk to the office which he had so far never managed in less than 10 minutes. Newcastle, like several other strategic parts of the world, had developed as a walled city so its offices and banks had sprung up on the high ground where the merchants traded safely within the fortifications. Every time he clambered the steep steps up to the walls he thought of the Royalists battling with Oliver Cromwell's besieging army. In modern times, the city fathers had tried, unsuccessfully, to operate lifts from the quayside to the city's giant Tyne Bridge, but had been beaten back by anti-social elements who abused them. So Sharpe made a climb to work every day that had gone on for centuries before.

He cut through Westgate Road with history all around him. He passed the Literary and Philosophical Society—one of the first public places to be lit by electric light—and in to Grey Street, the stunning Georgian architectural centrepiece of the city where The Metropolis had leased a massive first floor area above several stores, open planned and soundproofed it and kitted it out with rows of futuristic brightly coloured desks, bristling with computers, on pleasant magnolia carpets.

Huge televisions were suspended from the false, spotlight-infested ceilings. Live sports and news broadcasts would run silently alongside other screens full of teletext news services. The layout was open but crammed with table and desk workspace manned by reporters, sub-editors and photographers taking up around two thirds of the floorspace. The surfaces were adorned by countless desktops and all manner of newspapers and magazines. The floor was strewn with used newspapers awaiting collection by the office cleaners.

The walls of the office and the corridors feeding in to them were emblazoned at every turn with huge images of the Tyne and its numerous bridges, old and new, its museums, libraries and the coastline around the river. There was at least one huge image of Robert Morton on every wall, the media mogul cashing in on the Venezuelan tycoon's urge for anonymity at all costs by being the frontman for the venture.

As Sharpe entered the office he was almost knocked over by Tony Carver who was striding out, face slightly flushed, on his mission of the day. He glanced at him and smiled. "Hi young man. Glad you could make it. Phil's desperate for your help."

"What's going on?" He kept deadpan in the presence of the tall and portly veteran who had worked for national tabloids before settling for a quieter life in the English provinces and had more than 30 years in the industry behind him. One of the stories which Carver dined out on was how he was one of the first at the scene at the 1988 Lockerbie air crash disaster in Scotland. He had many a macabre story to tell of dead victims still strapped in their seat belts in broken-up sections of the plane.

Despite his wealth of experience, Carver was a dinosaur in the industry now and he knew it. He waxed nostalgic at the drop of a hat over the days when the telephone call box was the only friend a notebook-armed reporter had when he was out in the field miles away from base. The digital era had changed everything. Now every day brought him a new technology challenge such as how to capture video from an iphone and create a video blog or how to set up an RSS news alert. Sharpe, the new boy, had often had to help the old hand find his way around all this stuff.

Inside the office Carver felt trapped and stifled by sophisticated software, electronic gadgets and all the new digital gizmos. He was all smiles now as he was getting out of it for a while.

"Two death knocks. I am on one and Earnshaw is on the other. He needs someone to work the phones with us both out of the office. He's desperate for a decent story for the front of paper first edition and Chalmers is on his tail like a Rottweiller."

"Good luck then," Sharpe tried not to show his disappointment as he realised the reason behind the early morning call. He was to answer all incoming calls while the paper's more senior reporters were sent out to get the big stories of the day. At this time of day they would be mostly from reporters who worked areas outside the city checking in with their assignments for the day. Low man on the totem pole.

He crossed the office floor and Holmes waved him in to a seat by his side. The command desk was a huge, octagon-shaped table in the centre of the newsroom with places for all the executive staff, the news and picture editors and their deputies and the senior sub-editors. It had places for sixteen journalists and was usually fully staffed by midday but right now there were only a handful about.

"Need you on the phones George," Holmes rasped politely, his white face framed in heavy bi-focal spectacles. "My number two's away today and there's a couple of good possibles that I've had to gamble both the early morning lads on so I would like you just to hold things together while I go in to conference and set out my stall for the day."

Sharpe nodded assent and started rustling papers on his desk. It was not the time to grumble about being hauled out of his cozy bed for duties that had little dividend for a news reporter. Manning the phones didn't get you a byline in The Metropolis and he hoped he would not be kept too long on it. He looked at the huge diary on Holmes' desk. There were three news reporters expected in at 9 am and hopefully he would be assigned a story then and get out of the office.

Out of the corner of his eye, he studied the mess of items on Holmes' desk. There were at least eight newspapers in various states of dissection. There were nationals, there were regionals, there were small town newspapers with tiny circulations which somehow kept going from one year to the next. The local ones had been cut to ribbons as Holmes plundered other stories, public notices, lost and found columns and other sections for new story leads.

The one tidy part of his desk was reserved for the death notice columns which he and his deputy pored over every morning. These were always neatly cut out of the rival morning papers of their competitors and glued on to A4 sheets which Holmes shuffled incessantly as he searched for human disasters that would make good news stories.

It seemed unsavoury to Sharpe that the notices and tributes from loved ones which had been carefully worded and paid for to be placed in the death columns of newspapers as part of a public service, albeit a commercial one also, should be perused over in this fashion, at the nerve centre of the newspaper, by its editorial executives. The Metropolis called itself a family newspaper and opened its doors several days a week to guided tours of members of the public which were often groups of young schoolchildren. When Holmes was asked to welcome them and tell them about the role of the newsdesk, he would shuffle his newslist sheets expertly to disguise the death lists and show a BBC-style mix of stories of the day or maybe of the week.

The reality was that the Metropolis was like a news factory with a particular role, to be the first with the stuff that people talked about. And people tended not to talk about what the Prime Minister was doing for his country or what the economic outlook was. They tended to talk about sport, shopping and do you know what happened to whatshisname down the road? The death columns were where, more often than not, you first found out about the strangest and most horrible things that happened to people.

Many of the big picture and news stories which appeared in the national tabloids like the Sun and the Daily Mirror started off their lives as modest death notices in local papers. Death notices which contained a name, an age, an area, and the words "tragically" or "as the result of an accident" were seen as fair game. Behind these time-honoured words there could be all manner of stories.

Recent examples had been the body found in the boot of a car in the east end of the city which had become a murder inquiry; the tree surgeon who burned to death when the fire he had started down below, to throw branches on as he sawed, engulfed his tree; the head teacher who swallowed a bottle of pills after her school was slammed by Government inspectors.

It was the papers covering a large regional area, like the Metropolis in north east England and many other regionals throughout the country, which sniffed out these hard news stories and served them up first. There could often be lucrative spin-offs for them from syndication to the nationals.

Having found an item they wanted to investigate further in the death column of a newspaper, the next step was to find an address for the family of the poor unfortunate. This was usually done with the aid of the national electoral register which contained the names of all voters.

Sharpe was finding it hard to get used to how easy it all was to intrude on someone's grief. He had done a few death knocks for The Metropolis now and had found every one of them difficult. And he wondered if they would ever get easier. There were other sides to the job. There were courtrooms and there were council chambers where reporters were welcome to gather news. But the knock seemed the most important side of all. Sharpe wondered if it was the same on all city newspapers or whether it was just a strange mix of circumstances and individuals that prevailed in his office.

McNichol, Andy. 21, Newcastle. Died suddenly,
more information later . . . .

Death notices were always factual and brief but this was minimalist in the extreme. Tony Carver took one last glance at the sheet of paper in his hand before stuffing it in a coat pocket. He pressed the white ivory push button set in a small circle of brass which glared at him like a big dragon's eye. His stomach was uneasy before he pressed it and afterwards it swarmed like crazy. Deep down he hoped that the huge panelled front door would not be opened for him. He had been a long time in the job now and he was starting to prefer the easy way out, to pass the shit on to someone else down the line. Someone like Sharpe, the new boy in the officer who reminded him so much of how he used to be himself that he felt an urge to take him under his wing, a case of one misfit looking after another. Sharpe made Carver remember his own vulnerability when he first started in the job. Poor Sharpe was creative and a tabloid newspaper, even a small regional one in a city 300 miles north of Fleet Street, needed creative individuals like a drifting ship needed rocks. Once upon a time newspapers had been stepping stones for great writers, Charles Dickens for instance, but now they chewed them up. You had to write to a formula and learn fast just like he had. It was bash this out for deadline and go and find three other things for tomorrow. Constant pressure.

But it was better than working for a living, or so they said. Carver stared at the panels of the door. There had been minor attempts to deface the tired red paint which covered it, some initials and crosses scrawled by sweethearts and vandals with nothing better to do as they passed on the pavement. The house stood in the middle of a terrace of similar three-storey buildings and was of a size and in that part of the city which meant it would have been the home of a rich family in its heyday, would have endured the grief of two world wars before it took on a new life as three separate flats during the second half of the last century. Carver was sensitive to buildings. He felt happiest in bright modern ones like the open plan office of his newspaper with huge windows to let the daylight in and banks of modular lighting panels in the ceilings to combat the dark of winter.

This house was like a grumpy old man who had seen it all, had suffered bad times and got over them. It was a tired survivor in desperate need of architectural refreshment.

If there was no answer, he simply rang his boss and told him no go. His boss would moan a bit but pass on the message and the night duty man or woman would be sent out to try again to get an answer. He still so much hated this part of the job despite having refined an ability to deal with every nuance of doorstep behaviour.

Each residential unit had a different story to tell, judging by the windows. The fascia of the top flat smacked of dereliction. The exterior of the ground floor was flaky and encrusted with dirt but inside it had nice silk curtains. The first floor flat was different. Its large sash windows were freshly painted and boasted window boxes with begonias and herbs. It was cared for. It was like someone was trying to give the building a smile and put lipstick on it. The inhabitant of this flat was Carver's mission for the morning.

Somewhere deep inside there was a slight noise of movement which started to get louder. He gulped and waited, trying not to frown at the fact he may not have an easy way out. His heart quickened as the door swung slowly open to reveal a harmless looking white-haired man in thin black spectacles and a crumpled dressing gown with a hint of crumbs from his morning toast on it.

The man gazed blankly at him and Carver showed him his i.d. card. He spoke quickly but softly and smoothly: "Sorry to bother you sir. I am from The Metropolis newspaper. You may have heard of us. We are quite new to the city."

He tried to sound a chirpy as usual. Why be too serious and pompous, like some of the new kids, or disguise his own friendly nature? He waited as the man's eyes focused on his card and slowly, carefully absorbed all the information on it. The card said: Tony Carver, reporter, The Metropolis, Newcastle. Below this a message: All the news am to pm as it happens.

The man blinked again, looked at him now with a hint of anger. He had sturdy shoulders and red cheeks. He looked like a man who could have a temper if aroused but his eyes were full and Carver felt his body relaxing as he recognised he was dealing with a man lost in grief. It was something he encountered quite a lot. It often made his job easier.

"I don't want to talk about it. Please just . . . ."

Impending failure. Carver tried to make his voice lighter, his presence less foreboding. Carver was just under 6ft tall but towered over the smaller man. He was also large in the girth due to spending less time at his health club and more at his local pub. He was crouching now as he sought to speak with a tone that said he understood.

"Sir. Would you not like to pay tribute to your son, to let people know what a fine man he was? I gather he was popular, well spoken of by his school and church."

Lies, all lies. All Carver knew was about the man's son was the information contained in the death notice stuffed in his pocket.

Another look that cut through him like a knife but then a change in the man's eyes. A glint of something else, pride maybe towards his dead son. Carver said nothing more. The man looked past him at the street as a milk float passed, the only sound to break the silence of the moment. He looked towards the clouds in the sky then back at Carver.

"Come in a minute."

Carver's hands went automatically for his notebook and pen as he crossed the threshold of the door.

Phil Holmes had the sort of face you usually found running casino tables. It was white and unhealthily spotty but unflappable. It was ideal for its purpose which was to be news editor of a large circulation city newspaper. At the moment this face was trying to avoid the eyes of the editor of The Metropolis, who was prowling around the command desk like a shark assessing his next victim.

"I have a large bloody hole on the front page that is going to be claimed by the bloody Tory party conference if you don't give me a good local story. Come on team, what have you got?"

Gareth Chalmers was overweight and had the menacing gait of a school bully. He had all the sensitivity a drone missile reserved for a mujahideen and seemed to spend his life looking for targets to vent his aggression on.

"Come on Phil, what have you got?" Chalmers barked. "There's a million people out there. A large amount of them read what you guys write. Something must be happening to some of them. What's going on?"

Holmes sighed inwardly as he realised he was the one in the firing line. It was a bad day for the editor to be unsatisfied with the news content of the paper. If only he could have been away on some managerial mission. All the reporters had phoned in, one by one, between 7.30 and 8am to say there was nothing doing. Holmes knew what it was like. A news reporter's life was a sea of monotony on a daily basis until a rare incident, like maybe a murder, created that commodity called news. That was why news was news, because it was unusual and rare. It couldn't be prearranged like a game of football or tennis, events which made life so easy for the sports reporters. News was the unexpected, people who spent their lives being normal and boring suddenly finding themselves doing something outrageous or simply being in the wrong place at the wrong time.

But he couldn't say that to his editor. He couldn't say that because his editor's argument was irrefutable. There were a million people out there and the odds were that something odd or bad had happened to a couple of them in the last 24 hours. It was almost guaranteed. But there was also an army of people who didn't want reporters to know about it. There were the police chiefs who wanted it known that fear of crime was greater than actual crime itself and who let their subordinates know there had to be a bloody good reason for releasing news of a crime incident.

There were the fire and ambulance officers who were told to refer the press to the public relations department should they have inquiries and the public relations officers who saw their job as largely to confuse the press and form a barrier to their thrust for information. Holmes sometimes wondered how the paper ever got hold of a decent news story. He gazed in the direction of George Sharpe who seemed studiously buried in paperwork. He thought he saw his hand shaking slightly. Not good.

"I'm hoping for something from Tony Carver, Gareth. He's out on a death knock. He's good Tony. I'm hopeful. Earnshaw is out as well but he has a distance to travel. He won't make first."

"Ring him up now," Chalmers barked. "See what he's got, man! He's on the other end of a phone for God's sake."

Oh yes, Carver would love that right now, Holmes thought. The instruction from Chalmers showed just how little the newspaper's editor understood the world of the general news reporter and how sensitive an operation door-stepping could be. Persuading people affected by grief to open their hearts about it was a unique craft, one at which Carver excelled. He needed to be left to it.

Holmes knew that Carver must be at least in conversation with his target of the day as he would have been in touch by now to say he had failed. Holmes expected a call from his reporters just before a knock and immediately after with the result. In this way, with the seconds ticking towards deadline, he had an idea who would be bearing gifts to the altar of news and who would not. He felt Carver had the lucky touch although he would never say as much to anyone, least of all Carver, and Holmes, the man with the face of a professional gambler, was a career chancer whose gambles so far had come off more often than not.

"C'mon man, we need to know what it is. I need something big. I don't want another raggy on a motorbike today. Had enough of them lately."

"We'll have to wait Gareth. Tony will have his phone switched off now while he interviews. I can't give you any more information. It was a death notice in tonight's paper. A 21-year-old lad. No more than that."

A light flickered on the console on Holmes' desk. He was grateful for the excuse the call gave him to turn away from an editor on the warpath. Chalmers had been about to grill him some more but the telephone was king on the editorial floor and even interrupted editors in full flow.

Holmes curled his neck around the receiver while his eyes took in the Irish girl, a new face in the office, as she gathered papers from the printer. He was always intrigued by girls who dressed down for work, played it low key. He had grown disenchanted with the L'Oreal types who glistened and glowed their way around the newsroom jungle. The Irish girl walked back to her desk amongst the tidy rows of journalists' work stations. She disappeared from his view as he scribbled notes on his clipboard. The silence which engulfed the command desk was spreading throughout the editorial floor as staff waited to see if their editor, his face growing darker by the second, was going to explode.

Holmes put down the receiver and continued writing notes. Colleagues to his left and right were shifting in their seats. He finally looked up to meet Chalmers' eyes with the gaze of a man who had picked up a royal flush in a game of poker.

"That was Carver," he smiled. "Good man Carver."

Chalmers puffed out his chest like a huge pigeon.

"He has an interview with the father of a 21-year-old Northumberland fusilier killed in action in Afghanistan by the Taliban. He's a city man. Carver's on his way in with pictures, the lot. It's a whole package."

"Bingo." Chalmers trotted off to his sub-editors table as if he was bearing the Olympic torch. The command desk started emptying as its relieved occupants headed for the coffee machine.

Holmes' face bore a strange half smile now that Chalmers was off his back. He caught Sharpe staring at him. He could afford to smile at the newest recruit to the newsroom now.

Holmes shrugged his shoulders, grunted and started to tap on his keyboard. "The joy of death, eh?"

He had expected Sharpe to smile in mutual relief but instead found himself looking at a frowning face which seemed to question him—and he didn't like it.

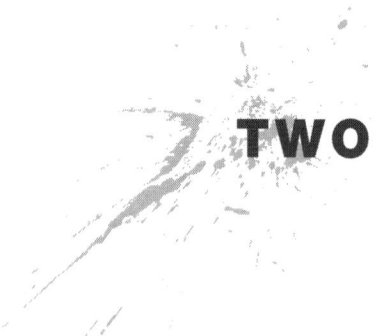

TWO

Wiliamson, Lisa, three, Morpeth, died tragically ....

Jeremy Earnshaw was a driven young man, a man who believed his job was not a popularity contest and was not interested in currying favour at any level below that of his boss. The more feathers he could ruffle around him, even amongst his own colleagues, the better. He was a skinny, belligerent, untrustworthy individual, the sort of reporter that some editors loved. He had an almost photographic memory and never put a foot wrong in stretching the truth of a story as far as it would go.

Jeremy Earnshaw was the future of The Metropolis because there was nothing about the future he feared. Simple notebook recording of events was finished. Photographers were finished. He was a multi-media man who could do it all . . . . words, pictures, videos. Technology was his tool and his huge doctor-style work briefcase brimmed with its accoutrements . . . . a mini-laptop, an ipad, microphones, minitapes, usb storage devices, flashdrives, spare phone cameras. He had spent a small fortune of his earnings on his accessories. He could turn a story from print to video in 20 minutes. His potential was infinite. They had all better watch out.

Earnshaw was even more motivated than normal on this particular morning as on the previous evening in The Rat, the pub near The Metropolis where all the journalists headed after work, he had been told in confidence of a new system by which its reporters were to be judged. His informant was Pete

Cowley, its deputy news editor. When he heard of the League of Death he expected to be top man on it. When he heard Tony Carver was top he hated him even more.

Jeremy Earnshaw had never liked Tony Carver from his first day on The Metropolis five months ago. Carver had taken him out on the rounds, introduced him to some police officers that might be helpful, taken him on a tour of the city courts. Carver was many years his senior and something of a legend in Tyneside news circles. So Jeremy Earnshaw hated him from that day on.

"Christ Pete," he wailed. "I'm better than him, got more results. The bloke doesn't even know how to make a video. He gets the shakes when he has to take a picture with his phone. He is past his sell-by date by a few years."

"He's painfully old school," Cowley agreed, "but that doesn't mean he's not good at what he does. The league doesn't lie and it says you're not better than him." Cowley patiently explained the points system to illustrate his case.

"You've done four death knocks this month so far with success on three. But you came back empty-handed on one, the lad who was gassed by the faulty flue in the gas fire in his flat, remember?"

Earnshaw didn't like being reminded of failure. The late reporter, Kirsty, had called out and got the story and pictures.

"There was no answer when I called. The house was empty."

"You could have tried the neighbours."

"I don't like doing that unless it's something really mega. The last thing you want is the person you want to interview getting home to be told by his neighbours that a reporter has been round asking questions. I like to catch people cold."

"I don't agree," Cowley interjected. "You have to squeeze the lemon to get the juice. No squeeze no juice."

"So you squeeze every lemon in sight?"

"Yes."

"Okay. I will get top of this list Pete. You can count on it."

Cowley smiled. "That's what I want to hear."

Earnshaw believed he had been given his chance next day when he was one of the two early men in to the office along with Carver. Phil Holmes had flashed a sheet of paper under his eyes. Earnshaw saw it was a photo copy of a death notice for a child, aged three. Lisa had already been traced through the register to Minewood, a village near Morpeth, in Northumberland, the uppermost county of England.

"I'm on the job now."

Holmes flashed another piece of paper. "There's your pool car chitty. Go for it."

Earnshaw headed purposefully for the lifts, past the rows of side-by-side desks shared by sub-editors each engrossed in their screens like a row of academics. The backroom boys, they called them. Earnshaw hated them as well.

On the ground floor he nodded to Eddie, the security man, and stepped through the entrance doors and walked over the road to the labrynth of elevated parking spaces inside the company garage. Getting one's allotted pool car out of the garage without a scratch on it was an art in itself but Earnshaw didn't worry too much about the odd scrape or scratch as he tooled it out. There were always plenty of marks on the cars allotted to journalists so what did a few more matter?

He navigated the city bus lanes, watching out for crazy taxi drivers, and then picked up the A1 heading for Morpeth. Within the half hour he was standing outside a modest terraced house in a one-time Northumberland coalmining village which had known better days.

The door was answered almost immediately by a softfaced woman. Earnshaw felt confident. He produced his ID card and made his pitch.

"My name is Jeremy Earnshaw of the Newcastle Metropolis. I wondered if you would care to talk to us about your loss."

The woman's face went blank. "I'm sorry. What do you mean?"

Earnshaw grappled with wordage. "Erm, the family notice in the paper tonight?"

"I'm sorry. I don't know what you are talking about. My wedding was in the papers five years ago but I can't imagine it's that."

"I'm sorry. I must have a wrong address," Earnshaw wanted to look again at the photocopied death notice in his pocket but knew it would be construed as tactless. He slipped his ID card back in his pocket. "Sorry to have bothered you."

"It's no bother. Would you like a cup of tea? You look stressed."

Earnshaw declined the offer and headed back to his car. Once in the driver's seat, he pulled the paper out of his pocket, checked the address scrawled in pen against it, and called Holmes on his mobile.

"Hi Jeremy, you got the big one for us? You've got big competition today. Tony's got nearly all the first edition news space with a war death."

"No, the right house might be a step in that direction Phil. Maple Street's a no no."

"Wrong address? I'll get somebody to do another search and get back to you."

Earnshaw sat back in his car seat and waited. If only he could have made the search himself. The electoral register always threw up plenty of names, some current and some out-of-date. They were narrowed down by location and guesswork. If there was just one name against an address, there was probably less chance of the parent of a child living there but you could never tell. Better to jot down all the potentials rather than plump for one, as in this case.

His mobile rang and he recognised the voice of Kirsty from the newsroom on the other end. She was a dark-haired, cheerful and attractive young woman who actually wanted to be a sports reporter but was only a couple of years in the job. Possibly because of her knowledge of sport, she was very popular in the Metropolis building. Earnshaw was determined not to like her. This feeling had been reinforced when Kirsty succeeded in getting a story which he had been given first shot at—a man who was gassed by a faulty flue to the gas fire in his flat. It was just luck, nothing else. There was nothing special about Kirsty.

"Try Orchard Street, number 57."

"You got a thing about trees Kirsty?" Earnshaw grumbled.

"No, what's the matter?"

"Well the last one was Maple Street. Were there any other streets nearby against the name of Williamson? I want them all."

"Well, I was just doing a best guess you know."

"Yeah well. Let me do the guessing and give me all the addresses."

Earnshaw was given a total of six addresses. He crossed out a couple and instead of heading for Orchard Street decided to try a Williamson a half a mile from the village centre on an outlying estate.

As he pulled the car to a stop, he noted the long shimmering row of white and silver condolence cards in the front bay window of the semi. A 4x4 stood on the drive. Bingo. He would be top of the list, he knew it.

The woman who answered the door had been crying which immediately worried him. No good to be upsetting her anymore. He didn't want yet another complaint about his doorstep manner. People had said he was cold and ruthless. He was trying to adapt a little.

"What do you want?" she said brusquely.

"Sorry to bother you, really really sorry. I'm from the Newcastle Metropolis and we wondered if you would care to talk about your loss, to pay a tribute to your daughter."

The woman's face softened.

"Well, I would, I really would. I loved her to bits. We are very private people though. I would have to know exactly what you are going to say. You can come in anyway."

Earnshaw gave the woman just the slightest of smiles, just enough to encourage her in her decision but not make light of the circumstances.

He stepped inside the opened front door ever so casually. The woman's hand pointed to a sofa and Earnshaw sought to sit down as quietly as possible and place his briefcase by his side. As he did so he noticed a family photo on the mantelpiece above the fire in the living room.

On the picture, Mrs Williamson was with her husband, Earnshaw surmised, and two small children, a boy and a girl. The smiling girl with freckles and wispy forelocks would be Lisa.

Earnshaw sat quietly putting the onus on Mrs Williamson to talk, and talk she did. With tears in her eyes, she spoke of how cruelly the disease of meningitis had robbed her of her baby girl and how the loss had shaken her to her roots but she was a believer and she believed it must all have been for a purpose at the end of the day.

Earnshaw quietly made notes in his spiral notebook as she told of the rush to hospital with the child after she noticed small spots on her skin, how she had done the glass test and the horror of realisation.

Jane and Bill Williamson, her husband of ten years, had dressed hurriedly and taken Lisa straight to the hospital. Bill had stayed in the family car with his son James, aged two, asleep on the back seat while his wife rushed in to the hospital carrying Lisa, who had become unconscious.

"The doctors were wonderful," she said with her eyes shining. "As soon as the doctors saw her, they knew straightaway they had to act and they did their very best. But it was God's will."

Earnshaw flipped the page of his notebook trying to make as little noise as possible as he scribbled notes. It was great that the woman was talking so freely. His interview was almost concluded. He had more information than enough now but there was one thing to complete the package.

"Mrs Williamson, can I ask you about the photograph over there?" he indicated towards the mantelpiece. "It's a very nice photo and that's Lisa, on the right, and her brother with you and your husband, yes?'

Mrs Williamson nodded and Earnshaw made a note in large letters in his book LISA, right of picture, and family. The two children were very young and he didn't want the sub-editors to make any mistakes. He would make sure it was written on the back of the picture when he handed it over for the front page spot.

"Can we borrow the photo for a day or two? We'll get it back to you. I will make sure I deliver it personally."

Mrs Williamson's face froze. A new look came in to her eyes. They became unfriendly.

"What for?" she demanded brusquely.

"Well, I think it will go nicely with the tribute piece we will put in the paper based on what you have told me this morning. She was a very lovely girl and it will be very nice."

Earnshaw suddenly felt things were going wrong. He tried to avoid Mrs Williamson's eyes as he leaned over and opened his briefcase.

"No, I'm sorry. I don't like the idea of Lisa's picture in the paper. My husband and I are very private people. We don't want to share family photographs with every Tom, Dick and Harry."

"Okay Mrs Williamson," Earnshaw spoke quietly, smoothly, trying to get her back in to the frame of mind she had been in before. "Thank you for talking to me and I always think this has all the answers when we are in this kind of situation."

Earnshaw pulled a large, bound bible out of his briefcase and stood up cupping it in both hands almost like a minister.

"The good book," Mrs Williamson beamed. "I shall be reading my own tonight. How nice that you carry it with you."

"I find it helps in the job."

"Of course, and thank you for your interest in my daughter."

"Thank you for talking to me."

Williamson moved quickly now as he sensed it was time for an exit. He placed the bible carefully in his briefcase and slowly headed for the door.

"Thanks again Mrs Williamson."

She watched him as he made his way back to the car. As he drove away down the street, she was still standing at the door.

THREE

As deputy news editor of The Metropolis, Pete Cowley had one overriding ambition—to replace Phil Holmes as its news editor. Cowley was a sporty, red-haired, fresh-faced media graduate, a "whizz kid" was the contemptuous description of him employed by his fellow hacks.

Cowley knew he wouldn't realise his ambition by just being the lapdog of the studious coffee-addicted Holmes. There had to be conflicts in judgement on key editorial decisions and he had to show he had a vision for The Metropolis. He had spent months agonising over this when the idea suddenly hit him out of the blue.

It happened on a slow news day which fortunately coincided with Chalmers, the editor, being at a media conference and his deputy, the Londoner Eddie Black, being indisposed through illness.

It was therefore a day when people could mentally put their feet up. Holmes was doing the Telegraph crossword and thinking of a job he could find for the Irish girl, something that would involve a lot of feedback between reporter and news editor, a way of getting to know her better. Cowley picked up a piece of A4 paper and printed on it, in large marker pen letters, THE LEAGUE OF DEATH.

He waved it to claim Holmes' attention but the poker face wasn't having any. Cowley continued with his work, writing the figure one and placing against the name of Tony Carver. The list continued with names until it was 10-strong. He waved it at Holmes again.

"What's the story?" Holmes sighed and threw his crossword page on to the pile of papers on his desk.

"It's The League of Death. I have just created it. What do you think?"

Holmes took the paper from him and gazed blankly at it. "The League of Death," he repeated.

"Yes, don't you see," Cowley waxed enthusiastically. "It's sometimes very difficult to work out shades of performance in our reporters. How do you judge rankings from top to bottom over, say, a period of a year to go towards an annual review, for instance?"

"Personally, I think it's bloody impossible. You can be a good reporter and have a bad run when you don't pick up good stories like a football striker who is not scoring goals."

Holmes was taken aback by the whoop of glee from beside him. "Exactly, that's the perfect analogy," said Cowley. "It's the league that ranks them. For a top striker it's the Premiership league that counts for everything. So we have a League of Death because that's what sells newspapers."

"Well, you know what Chalmers will say don't you?"

"Yes, have you got nothing better to do?"

"Yes, exactly.'

"Ah, c'mon Phil, a bit of light relief, you know."

"How can a league of death be construed as a bit of light relief?" Holmes inquired weightily.

"Well, it's the business isn't it? It's the business we are in. We are not kicking footballs."

Holmes smiled wearily. "Yes, nothing sells newspapers like death. That and the thought of the city's glorious football team actually winning a trophy for once. When I think of it like that, it makes us seem pretty pathetic really."

"Look," said Cowley, his voice turning serious. There was a strange almost fanatical gleam in his eyes. "There is a production line in tabloid newspapers, we all know it. It starts with the small town papers and works its way through the bigger city papers covering the larger industrial areas and ends up in Fleet Street and what's the common thread? The common thread is knocking on doors. ``It's where all the big stories are made, on the doorstep. Our kind of paper is a halfway house between the small and the huge. We are messengers swooping on every bit of misfortune we see on the screen, fax or in the classified columns, notably deaths. We are the link between the small and the big, we find the stories that grow like snowballs until they make the nationals."

Cowley dropped his voice as he realised the office had gone quiet. "So my league of death is like on a goals for and against basis based on the number of successful death knocks for each reporter."

He started drawing lines and columns on the paper. "See. It starts this month and it's early days yet. Carver is top because he, so far, has had three successful knocks."

"But so's Jeremy," Holmes pointed at the second name on the list, Jeremy Earnshaw.

"Yes but Jeremy has done four knocks, right, and on one he came back empty handed. He scores a minus one for that so he's only on two points."

Holmes, reluctantly, was becoming intrigued by the scoring system. It was almost amusing. "Jeremy came back empty-handed just the once because the house was empty. The night man, er, woman, got an answer, she got that story about the lad who was gassed by a faulty flue.

"Yes, good story, but the point for that goes to Kirsty. She got the story, puts her in fifth position with one point."

Holmes squinted at the list again through his black Buddy Holly glasses. "So there's four reporters with one point each in the list. How come she's the top one amongst them?"

Cowley's face was so serious that for a moment Holmes wondered about his sanity.

"Because she made the front page. It goes in order of placing in the paper. Gareth only made page two and Emily and Jane were page five and page seven respectively."

"Road accidents. Ten a penny."

"Exactly, so you see my system gives each reporter a ranking which exactly equates to his performance."

"But it only applies to death knocks. What about all the other aspects of the job? Interviews with celebrities, local politics, magistrates' courts, crown courts, sport, all the other blah, blag blah things?"

A silence dropped between the two men. It lasted a minute until Cowley broke it.

"Unusual death sells newspapers like nothing else," he said tersely. "It's The League of Death."

Cowley was like a man who had been possessed by a spirit. He was stone cold serious and he hadn't finished.

"We could develop it more with a more complex points system, you know like in the Premiership, three for a win, one for a draw and zero for a loss."

"What on earth would count as a draw?" Holmes asked incredulously.

"If a reporter goes on a death knock, gets an answer at the door, but, after trying all his powers of persuasion, he cannot coax an interview out of the family, he might merit a point."

"In other words, a no comment."

"Yes, exactly. There's a fair level of stress in no comments. You are trying to get someone to talk and they are not responding. It's all journalistic energy wasted. Much different to a straight no."

Holmes shook his head unbelievingly. "Fuck me Pete," he growled. "It's not Match of the Day. If you want to do this, keep it simple."

Cowley nodded feebly, realising he had gone too far.

"And it has to get the nod from above," Holmes stipulated, comforting himself with the knowledge that it never would.

FOUR

Sharpe walked the damp cobbled lanes running up from the bridges and pubs of the quayside with brisk purpose. The sun danced on his face like a stranger wanting to know him. The rain seemed to have lasted a whole fortnight and as he came in to the city centre there was a noticeable buzz in the air. The steps surrounding the city's central landmark, the Earl Grey monument, were full of people, tourists and tramps, speakers with a message about how to achieve redemption or how capitalism had to be defeated, and smokers on break time. Earl Grey stood proud and aloft above it all, a symbol of rich history now surrounded by faceless shopping malls. Commuters flooded in and out of the Metro station gateways, A few traders had pitched stalls to catch their attention. They were selling fruit, leather bags, some French goods and farm produce. Early March and spring was in the offing after months of rain and floods. The greyness of the city was lifting and people were talking cheerfully .

The kitchens were starting work in Chinatown and he savoured the melange of delicate flavours as he walked along Stowell Street. He cut through by the remains of one of the medieval walls which straddle Newcastle and contribute to its strange mix of ancient and modern and clocked a beggar lurching towards him. He found a coin in his back pocket and shoved it at the man, a druggie who was a familiar face in that area. He shuffled away and he studied his grey and pink charity shop clothes and trainers, old Primark with a splash of Sports Direct.

By the time he reached the Percy he was slightly out of breath. He noted that he still hadn't managed to beat Mary who was already in a corner of the bar with a Guinness and a newspaper in front of her. He got himself a pint of lager served by a cheerless barman and joined her.

"Howdy handsome," came the greeting delivered in crisp Belfast tones. "And what's your fettle?"

"I'm good. It's a lovely day and I have no complaints, not yet anyway."

"Plenty of time for complaints. Me, I'm planning a St Patrick's Day menu. Not long now, just a week or so."

"Planning a menu for St Patrick's Day? Thought it had to be Irish Stew."

"Not so, Sherlock," Mary was chirping, and almost licking her lips, as she enjoyed her favourite subject of food. "There are others. Corned beef and cabbage for instance, shepherd's pie and Irish soda bread. And I once had fish and chips on Paddy's Day."

"You devil. It's just the peasant in you, isn't it?"

"Then there's Colcannon, is a traditional Irish dish mainly consisting of mashed potatoes with kale or cabbage. It is also the name of a song about the dish."

"Okay enough of peasant food. You're making me hungry. And the smell of Chinatown is getting to me as well."

"Shall we go? The Bamboo is supposed to be excellent."

"I suppose. I could wait a little." Sharpe unbuttoned his coat gazing momentarily at the beer pot he was trying to get rid of. He thought of the pizza he had enjoyed the night before and felt guilty. Then he thought of the monthly leisure club payment he made and his lack of use of the facilities. He frowned and ran a hand through his hair throwing the thick front locks backover. Mary sat cross-legged studying her tights as she waited to hear whatever was itching him. They were the only two people in the bar apart from the barman who was now choosing his horses for the day, face buried in a tabloid and rambling quietly at the mouth.

"You know Mary, my dad worked in timeshare once in a place called Portimao on the Algarve coast of Portugal," Sharpe confided mysteriously. "He used to call you lot tinkers."

Mary's face hardened. "You mean he called the Irish people tinkers, he categorised us as itinerant travellers."

"No," Sharpe wagged his head and grinned. "he was trying to sell timeshare and whenever he tried to get an Irish person to splash their cash he said he would always get the same answer."

"What?" Mary was bristling, ready for a verbal scrap.

"Oi'll have to tink about that."

She burst in to laughter and then slapped him on the shoulder. It was playful but quite a heavy slap.

The barman glanced across the room at them and they became quiet.

Sharpe became serious. "You know Mary, you're the only person I work with that I could say this to but I'm uneasy in my job."

Mary tried to stay light. "Oh dear. You and me, we've both been on the paper now for how long, all of a few months no less. It's too long. We need a change. Let's try the armed forces. I've always fancied firing a rocket launcher myself. At least Afghanistan will be warmer."

His stare was almost apologetic but he was not going to change course. "Now then, I suppose you're right. It's a shame to be serious on a day like this but I thought you might understand, might know where I am coming from."

"Go on then, try me."

"Well, the thing is that I went in to journalism because I wanted to write. I like messing around with words. I like writing. But working for The Metropolis, you don't get a chance. Everything is already written in their bloody heads, the sub-editors', that is. And it's mostly about death. Fucking road accidents, murders, drownings, drug deaths, freak deaths, mystery deaths. It's all they want and it's depressing."

"I don't suppose we're going to pick up a Nobel prize for what we're doing at the moment George. But we have to start somewhere. I look at myself as being in a sect that slaughters beasts for the Gods, the Gods being the tabloids. Our purpose is to keep the Gods happy with choice dead offerings."

"I'll drink to that," said George, "but I don't for the life of me understand you."

His flippancy disguised the fact that he was stunned for a moment as he tried to assess whether Mary was serious or not. She was. "That must be an Irish Catholic thing," he said. "A dead offering? Headless man found in car boot. That sort of dead offering."

"Exactly. That might have started off in a small weekly paper's death column, died suddenly or something, just like loads of others, but by knocking on doors and asking questions about all these daily death notices we killed a lot of rubbish and offered up a worthy specimen for the Gods of newsprint."

Silence engulfed the pair. He realised Mary had opened her heart to him but it left him wondering about her. Up to now he had believed she was the only sane person he knew in a crazy world. He decided to persevere.

"But that's just it. Holmes, Cowley, Carver, they are all obsessed with death and the death notice announcements in the classifieds. I thought they would be wordsmiths but they are not. Like, my heart still beats to the printed word. They are heartless. They have merciless little engines that run on printer's ink. Where's the next Charles Dickens going to come from when newspapers are like this? I mean the greatest English writer after Shakespeare was a reporter before he was a writer."

"Aye, in the days that people read short stories."

"In the days that newspapers published short stories and good writing. I spent half a day doing a pen portrait of Newcastle and its interesting characters a month ago and it's never been used."

"Dickens married an editor's daughter also. Perhaps that helped."

"That's a bit cynical Mary. He was famous in his own right."

"Or in his own write, like John Lennon. I can't get in to Dickens. I read mostly Irish authors, good old James Joyce at the minute."

"Now John Lennon, there's a writer, albeit of songs. His output was phenomenal. Lennon and his band from the backstreets of Liverpool took over the music industry, put America in its place."

"Oh, really."

"Yes, just four young lads. From 1963 to 1969 they ruled. Pure creative drive. Some would say they still rule now."

"So how do you know so much about the Beatles?"

"Oh, my dad. He is a Beatles fanatic. He saw them live at Portsmouth Guildhall in 1963. He was 17 and he's been talking about them ever since."

"What made you do business studies George if you're so fond of books and arts and culture and everything?"

"Oh, my dad and his three brothers. The three wise uncles. I wanted to do English Literature but they bent my head in to something more practical. They said writing and that sort of stuff had to be a sideline. I sometimes wish I had never listened."

The conversation turned back to work and Mary's tone became softer as if she was dealing with a slow learner . He didn't like this but he listened, enjoying the sparkle in her eyes and the way her blonde bob moved as she talked.

"I think we have to be a bit patient," she said. "You know we're both in the same position you and I. We have both done a year or two on smaller papers and now we're working for regional ones. You have to think it's kind of a halfway house. We're like a supply line for the nationals aren't we? The Mirror and The Sun wouldn't have any nasties without we first dug them up."

Sharpe gazed suspiciously at Mary. "You sound like them, like Holmes and Cowley and the rest of the dickheads."

"Dickheads? You are in a bad fettle aren't you. They are just hacks, plain and simple."

"Yes, hacks that write all day about nasties, murder, mayhem, misery, and everything with a capital Death."

"Well you know it sells papers."

"So they keep telling me. But I'm uneasy. I don't want to be knocking on the door of some dad just hours after he's lost his teenage son in a road smash."

"But it's life and we can't report life unless we knock on doors George. The death knocks have to be done. That's how we find the real belters that make the nationals."

"If you say so Mary, but I thought you might understand my argument. I mean we are calling on people in grief and they're mostly not expecting us. We have no authority. There's no code. I don't think it's right. And we have to get them to sort of sign up to a package while they are in grief. You know, a nice family picture of the deceased and a lot of juicy quotes about him or her. It reminds me of what my dad used to say about timeshare selling. To be successful you had to keep your customer hot, keep him talking, keep him in the room, keep the dialogue going, and close the deal then and there, get him to pay the first instalment. He used to hate it but he had to do it. We're doing the same thing aren't we, closing the deal, in and out of somebody's house with what we want and then Ça ne fait rien."

"You don't need authority or a code to knock on someone's door George. It's a free country and it's full of streets full of doorbells and knockers. If we don't do it we don't get the stories. And people don't have to talk to us. They can close the door on us."

" Yes, but that's where we use all our skills to persuade them not to. What right do we have to be there? Is there any other job in the world that is so objectionably intrusive?"

"We can do it because we are unique. We have earned that unique right as trained observers, if you like, to occupy spaces that other people simply cannot. I suppose the obvious example is the war correspondent. He goes virtually anywhere with just his press badge for protection."

"You know as well as I do that those people we work for read the newspaper death notices every day and hand out jobs accordingly. It's disgusting."

"So you say." Mary giggled and swigged on her Guinness. Her eyes flashed mischievously at him from beneath her cropped hair. "Maybe you're right. Maybe it's all total crap. The gospel according to George Sharpe is the only truth."

"Well thank you. We've talked round this so much I can't tell if you're serious or not."

"Surely, and that will be my mystery. Hey, I don't know if I should tell you this George. It might not make yer day but do you know about the League of Death."

"The League of Death. What is this, a star chamber or something?"

Mary looked thoughtful. "Do you fancy Chinatown?."

"Yes," he said. "Let's live it up."

It came as a surprise to Sharpe that Mary Rainwell wanted to be an editor but she explained it all to him matter-of-factly over king prawn chop suey in the Bamboo, interrupted now and again by an over attentive Chinese waiter.

"Well, I think why not? And why not now? The Metropolis is so macho. Have you worked out the ratio of male to female reporters?"

"Four to one?"

"That's about right. It can't possibly stay that way not the way things are going. The paper needs a bit of girl power and I'm the one to provide it. I can see my route as well."

Sharpe was left in envy of Mary's clarity of purpose. He noticed how her eyes sparkled as she talked about her plans and the way she mapped them with her forefinger on the tablecloth.

"Look, there's Holmes there. He's a good news editor, a sensible decision maker. He has to progress. There's only one place he can go, deputy editor."

"What about Eddie Black?"

"Eddie's a Londoner. He had to leave his family to come up here last year to get that job. It's a stepping stone for him. He will go back to London."

"So where do you come in?"

"I go in as deputy news editor when that smarmking Cowley takes over the news desk. I do that for a year then I switch to the sub-editor's table and then I turn the screws."

"I don't get this. What screws?"

"Aha, that's where my Irishness comes in. Think about it."

Sharpe sat transfixed in thought. He clicked his fingers. "Of course, the managing director. She's from Ireland."

"Yes, catholic Ireland and all."

"I see it all. You state your case to her for a woman's touch and she finds some kind of special job for you, assistant editor or something."

"Exactly, then two years and I'm back to Ireland to take on an editor's job. Want to come?"

"Only if I can write a meaningful column."

"Maybe," Mary flashed a smile and they chinked glasses.

Lunch with Rainwell had left Sharpe slightly drunk from the bottle of wine they had shared. He had drunk most of it. She had someone to meet and they parted company with respectful kisses on the cheek.

He called in a Starbucks and ordered a latte. Here there were people reading books. He felt at home as he scanned what was being read. One of the patrons was reading Dostoevsky, Crime and Punishment. She had to be either East European or a literature student, he surmised.

After the coffee, he made his way across Northumberland Street, the city's shopping centre, which was busy as ever. When he reached the W.H. Smith store he saw a familiar face staring at him from its display window. Geoff, his best friend through a previous life now making a name for himself in stand-up comedy. The irony. His old classmate now making big strides in the world from the most unlikely of starting blocks. Not so long ago Geoff had been working in a call centre for an unspectacular wage. Now he was closing in on the big time on the strength of two-line jokes written on the Metro train to work and his first DVD was staring at Sharpe from the window.

It had taken him years of effort to become a journalist, years of sailing against the wind, of enduring the upraised doubting eyebrows of tough editors, of ignoring the well-meaning cozy advice of family members who knew what was best for him, of bypassing the sensible entreaties of teachers, of side-stepping careers advisers, of snubbing best friends, including Geoff who may have given him the best advice of all.

"If you want to write, go down to London and get involved with other writers, get on the doorstep of the publishing houses. Don't be a hack. Hacks aren't writers. They mostly are the subservient messengers of society, hunting in packs for information because as individuals they are weak, dominated by editors who suppress their wages and worth and who are in turn dominated by corporate businessmen who rule the roost. You might as well write a blog. Newspapers have had their day. Join them and it will kill you"

He had ignored it and gone his own way, prevailed against a tide of opposition, not the least from the newspaper industry itself which for a long time did not seem to want him. Interview had followed interview and he had driven his old Ford the length and breadth of Britain trying to make a break in to newspapers. Finally it was down to the veteran editor of his home town newspaper, a man who was shielded by a secretary called Peggy, who could scare a bear, that it came about.

A year of small town newspaper work, trudging around police press rooms, court and civic chambers, and the constituency office where Labour had been voted in time after time since World War 2, was enough to severe any loyalty he might have felt to Jim Chambers, the sexagenarian editor who had given him his break, and he was able to get a job with The Metropolis.

So what would Geoff say now? He had a nondescript car and a nondescript flat but they both presented bills that had to be paid and, worst of all, was he actually being seduced by the whole macho bullshit of newspaper work, of going out and banging down doors and barriers to be first with the news?

A driving force in the whole structure of the newspaper he worked for was egotism, be it of the male or female variety. So many egos wanting to be satisfied that they were definitely the best at what they did. It didn't matter if what they did verged on the criminal—if it achieved success it was a means to an end. "Don't let the facts stand in the way of a good story." This was one of the first things you were told by older hacks. It was a joke but it wasn't a joke.

Most of the people he knew followed this principle. It was what Jeremy Earnshaw did every day of his working life. He had seen Jeremy in action, coaxing information and then bending it like a welder forming a shape out of a piece of iron. It had to be of a certain shape and form to fill the space.

All he needed to know to get by in writing news stories could be gleaned in just six months, keep sentences tight, kill off superfluous words, use a bright intro. Then just write.

Plus a little bit of law. But they were always giving refresher courses in the law anyway, because they thought you were thick and they didn't want expensive law actions against them, so it was easy to keep abreast of it.

It annoyed him that fat chefs, ignorant wannabe celebrities and immoral sportsmen were the icons who filled the shelves of this bookshop. And his friend Geoff and an assortment of other standup comics were amongst them. He went in to the store and flicked through Geoff's book. It was a load of drivel about his early life, school holidays, girlfriends. He was thankful that he didn't appear to be mentioned in it. On the back of the book was a short piece about Geoff in which he was described as a comedian and writer.

A writer? You could write all that Geoff had ever written in the notes section in a pocket diary. A red mist was engulfing Sharpe. He was angry and he was going to vent his anger in the bookstore.

He marched past the cashier tills and found a customer service desk at the back of the shop. A young, dark-haired woman with a thin serious face was in charge.

"Can I speak to the manager."

The woman looked up from a sheet of paper she had been studying and eyed him carefully. "The manager, sir? Can't I help?;

"This is a matter for the manager." Sharpe gave her a deadly serious face, one to match hers. He kept his tone calm and convincing. "I'm from the inspection board."

"The inspection board?" the woman's eyebrows shot up. "What inspection board?"

He raised his eyebrows in mock surprise. "You haven't heard of the inspection board? Have you heard of the Civic Centre?"

"Yes, the council HQ. I'll just go and get him," the woman threw up her arms in a signal of defeat. She disappeared through a back room of the store. Several minutes later a man in a blue suit, perspiration on his brow, appeared. "Hello, what's all this. How can I be of help?"

"Sir, I want to take issue with your front window display. It's not a balanced display. It is full of low standard books which will be forgotten in a couple of years. You need some classics in there. Have you heard of Charles Dickens?"

"Well of course I have heard of Charles Dickens," the manager's tone was exasperated but he remained polite.

"He wrote about debt and poverty and how it affected ordinary people and his writing is as relevant today as it was then."

"I daresay but it's not my job to worry about that."

"Have you heard of Dostoevsky who wrote about people living in troubled times, most notably Crime and Punishment?"

"Well, yes, as a matter of fact, and he wrote The Idiot, as I remember, and I am beginning to think I am dealing with one. What do you want? What is this inspection board?"

"It's a new concept aimed at getting bookshops to balance their window displays. Yours is full or rubbish, standup comics, the ramblings of WAGs and wannabes, fat chefs. Have you ever heard of the angry young man? He hasn't got a place on your bookshelves and the world needs some angry young men right now, literate ones that is. And angry young women."

The manager picked up a telephone and started dialling a number. Tailford heard a deep voice at the other end. "Market Street police station."

"Hey, there's no need for that. I'm from the Civic Centre."

"Well then, you won't mind me checking that out with the local crime centre will you?"

A couple of young assistants were now at his side nudging him in the direction of the exit door. Sharpe pushed them back as he tried to make a dignified exit.

"That's right, get lost. You will be arrested if you're still here when the police come." The manager had come round from behind the shop counter and was in his face.

Sharpe ran for it.

FIVE

Cowley was already starting to claim results for his new system.

"It's getting them going. It's creating more competition between them."

Holmes didn't like this. He had agreed the promotion of the over eager Cowley from the ranks of the reporters just two months ago and didn't like him having ideas yet. He, Holmes, was the ideas man. He wanted Cowley to translate HIS ideas in to action not come up with his own. He just wished Cowley would get the picture.

Holmes' soured face lifted slightly at the sound of Mary Rainwell who was passing the desk on her way to the coffee machine. Such was the crammed nature of the editorial floor that it was difficult to get to the coffee machine without passing the command desk. Reporters suspected it was engineered this way so they would always be easy to observe. The concept of open plan had been used by management to make them all seeing and all powerful.

"I don't know why you guys don't just run a tote on your little league table as well. We could all have a flutter."

Her Irish brogue caught the attention of Holmes immediately. His head lifted. He smiled. His eyes looked out pleasurably on the shapely form of the latest recruit to the office. Not dressed to kill. Dressed to work but still eye catching nevertheless. Mary was slim and fresh faced with sparkly blue eyes and a mischievous grin.

"Hey, might do that. Fancy a punt?"

"No way, I'm saving up for a car. I want a BMW, a Z4."

"Ah, a journalist with a top-of-the-range car. How you going to do that?"

"You watch me. I won't be paid peanuts for too long. I'm telling you."

Holmes grunted to himself as he had to break off the conversation to deal with the phone that was flashing its pickup light in front of him. The voice on the other end was female and anguished, choking back sobs.

"It's Mrs Williamson here. Your reporter came to my house."

"Hello Mrs Williamson. Just looking at my list," Holmes spoke slowly playing for time and gazing at Mary Rainwell as she disappeared towards the coffee machine. He flipped a switch to cut the connection and caught Cowley's eye. "What's the position with that meningitis girl?"

"First class. It's all through and with the subs, whole package, nice picture. I also had a sidebar done by the health reporter about the killer disease of meningitis."

"Any idea why this woman might be ringing? She sounds very upset."

"Can't say I have. Jeremy said it was all straightforward."

Holmes flipped the switch back. "Hello Mrs Williamson, sorry to keep you. How can I help?"

Things were no better. The woman was still choking back sobs. Holmes had an awful feeling that things were about to go pear-shaped.

"I've been robbed. A photograph has been taken from my mantelpiece. A photo of me and my family. Your reporter is a thief."

Holmes' stomach started churning. "Hang on a minute Mrs Williamson. Jeremy reported back with the information about your daughter and the picture and, if I may say so, there's a very nice, respectful story about Lisa going in the paper tonight."

"But I said no picture. I told him we're very private people. I'm fine about a story but no picture."

"I see."

"I'm not stupid. I have a relative who wants to be a journalist. I know about the press code of conduct and all that kind of thing. I want that photograph back and I don't want you to use it."

Mrs Williamson slammed down the phone. Holmes gazed at the large digital clock display which hung from the newsroom ceiling and saw there was five minutes to deadline. He breathed a sigh of relief as he realised there was still time to pull the picture.

Mary Rainwell was marching his way with a coffee in either hand. He put a hand on her waist and guided her to his seat. "Mary, watch the phones love. I need to do something quick."

He swooped towards the sub-editors' table like a guided missile. Chalmers was standing over his team studying the story list, looking very self-satisfied.

"Er, Houston we have a problem," Holmes tried to sound upbeat.

Chalmers gazed at him impatiently.

"This front lead. Mrs Williamson has just been on the phone playing hell."

"Oh no," Chalmers gazed away in to the distance.

"She says no authority was given for the photo. It was taken without her consent. We'll have to pull it."

"Okay Phil."

"Okay."

Holmes felt vindicated but unwanted. He wandered back to his desk. As he faded in to the distance Chalmers turned to his chief sub.

"Damned if I'm pulling it now. Just run it Dave."

Dave Smithson glanced nervously at his editor. He thought of querying the wisdom of the action. He looked around the table at the other subs who were all looking at him. Not a word was spoken.

"Yes boss."

When Holmes got back to his desk Cowley was waiting for him with some news.

He had tried to think of a way of putting it delicately but given up.

"You know that Irish lass has got the hots for Sharpe don't you?"

Holmes laughed. "You're joking. She's much too smart for him. She will be mine, I tell you."

SIX

Chalmers liked Eddie Black because he was, to all intents and purposes, an alien in that sphere of the newspaper world which they both inhabited.

Black had spent the best part of his 20 years in newspapers forging a name for himself in London. From leaving school he had joined a small weekly as office boy. Several years had passed before he was able to seize an opportunity to get on the editorial floor as a trainee reporter. He worked his way up to the news desk on the Evening Standard.

He was still thrusting upward on his way to becoming an editor when he decided on a move out of his beloved London. He had nothing to lose. He was still the right side of 40 and had not yet found a woman worth settling down with despite some close calls. He was offered and took the deputy editorship at The Metropolis and he had regretted it ever since. Every stage of the long journey north up the M1 had left him feeling more like a fish out of water. The midlands of England offered no solace. In Yorkshire he found it difficult to communicate, to understand and be understood. In Newcastle he found it almost impossible to decipher the Geordie dialect, a northern England vernacular so confusing to Black that he often had to ask people to repeat their words. It was a lonely world he inhabited and he longed to be able to head back down the M1 to watch West Ham but, as a newcomer, he was expected to work a lot of Saturdays. He seemed to spend more time in the office than anyone else, particularly Chalmers, who was never seen at weekends. When he raised the matter with Chalmers he was told that Saturday was a quieter day and a good day for picking up on how to run the paper.

There was absolutely no chance of Black ever becoming accepted by the northerners who made up the captaincy of The Metropolis. They would listen politely to his meanderings about his studies at the University of Life and the decisions he had grappled with in his London days and then completely leave him out of the decision-making process on the stories of the day. He was the Banquo's Ghost of the editorial conference. Only Chalmers ever saw him. No-one had ever asked him if he was enjoying himself and he wasn't a person who gave his feelings away freely.

So he was an alien and that was why Chalmers liked him. He would not, could not conspire with anyone behind his back. He could not argue powerfully in editorial conferences so that the thrust of editorship was all from Chalmers. He had no allies. To Chalmers the sound of Black's irritating cockney twang was just sweet music.

Chalmers wanted this state of affairs to continue so he tried to find little roles for Black that would make him feel important, staff surveys, liaison with other departments in the city centre offices of The Metropolis, social events.

When Black came to him muttering something about a performance related league table that might enhance the work ethic on the The Metropolis he was much too busy wrestling with the stories of the day to take much notice. He decided to just give him carte blanche to go ahead after hearing he had been talking to Pete Cowley about it.

"If it's any good you can throw in a monthly prize. There's a load of champagne still in storage from when the team lost that tournament final in Japan a couple of years ago that needs to be used."

Black beamed and took the news back to Cowley who was delighted.

"Prizes," Cowley told Holmes smugly. "They're going to give prizes."

Holmes looked up quickly from the news list he had been buried in.

"Prizes for what?" he demanded.

"The League of Death," Cowley declared triumphantly. "It's official. A bottle of champagne to the winner each month. How good is that?"

Holmes groaned and rose from his desk. He cut a dejected figure as he headed towards the small office of Liz Saunders, Chalmers's secretary, which was effectively an ante-room to the editor's.

"Can I see Gareth please?"

"Mr Chalmers is busy. He's asked to not be disturbed."

Holmes left her talking to herself as he opened the door in to Chalmers' office. Chalmers looked up irritated, about to bark something. Holmes met his gaze with a calculated indifference. It worked.

"Okay, there must be a reason why you've barged your way in."

"Yes, it's the death list."

"What death list?"

"This League of Death that Pete Cowley dreamed up. It's potential dynamite."

"What are you talking about?"

"The League of Death that you've sanctioned. It's like a death knock premiership table. If the watchdogs of the press ever find out about this it'll be like phone hacking and Rupert Murdoch."

"The cockney arsehole said it was a performance-related table."

"Perhaps you should have looked at it properly."

"Well he's so bloody harmless I decided to give him his head."

"Might be your head at the end of the day."

Chalmers paused and looked carefully at Homes. Then he smiled serenely.

"I don't know about it, okay? What I don't know about can't harm me. If anything happens, it's Black's head, okay? What you have just said to me never happened okay."

"Okay." Holmes knew it was time to leave. He backed out of Chalmers' office and managed to avoid the withering gaze of Liz Saunders as he made his way back.

As a reporter on The Metropolis, Mary Rainwell had expected to find herself out and about on the streets of Newcastle and its surrounding neighbourhoods interviewing people about a wide variety of things, meeting them over lunch in trendy bars and restaurants, hobnobbing with the glitterati of the city at nightspots.

But no, she was expected in to the office at 7am every day to sit at her desk awaiting the dispensations of Holmes and his sidekick Cowley who ruled over their roost of around 20 news gathering reporters with the manner of teachers trying to keep control of a disorderly class. Mary had always thought it would be glamorous working in a spacious open plan newsroom with the latest in cutting edge technology. But somehow the organisation of The Metropolis made it oppressive. Staff were too close together and there was a general feeling of being watched and observed constantly. Then there were the short lunch breaks and no expenses. Mary had been told by an old hand that the golden days of boozy lunchtimes on expenses had all gone. Everything was on a shoestring these days.

It was hard work getting made up for a day at the office at the crack of dawn. Mary took great pride in her appearance and the task of doing herself up was difficult enough at that time of day without the added burden of Emma, her roommate in the cramped Tyneside flat, who worked flexitime for a city finance firm and usually slept late and worked late meaning that Mary had to pick her way quietly around the flat. Washing her hair was a nightmare with the faulty shower which always ran cold when you least expected it. Mary suspected her roommate used up all the water with her leisurely evening bath after returning from work.

All that work to get there presentable for 7am and then wait for either Holmes or Cowley to come sidling up with her job for the day nearly always in the form of a cutting from the death notices. They used office razors to cut up the back pages of the paper but were pretty messy with it. Then she would go out in a grubby pool car to her destination of the day.

Today was St Patrick's Day. It made her homesick to think of her mates in Belfast who would all be preparing for a big night out. She had bought food and drink for the evening but somehow it was not the same. And the St George's Day lot were having none of it, just a little smile of acknowledgement when she mentioned it to Holmes and then he came up with a job for her. She had a female intuition that Holmes liked her but he had a poor way of showing it. He had sent her out to follow in the footsteps of Jeremy Earnshaw who she didn't like. She had only met him once in the local pub all the reporters frequented after the day's work but she got dreadful vibes from his sweaty handshake. She had heard he had no scruples whatsoever in his dealings with either colleagues or readers. She decided to steer clear of him.

Holmes had asked her to make a second call on the house, a little semi on a small housing estate in the Morpeth area. There was a silver 4 x 4 on the drive and lots of white condolence cards which could be clearly seen in the bay window.

Mary strode quickly up the drive. She took a deep breath as she pressed the doorbell. She hated this part of the job but everyone reckoned it had to be done, apart from George Sharpe.

Jane Williamson's mood was lifted when she opened her front door to a vivacious young woman with flowing blonde hair, engaging brown eyes, and looking effortlessly smart in a black riding jacket and soft skinny jeans.

She smiled for the first time in days but then her face froze as her eyes fastened on to the bright green ballerina shoes which were totally at odds with her outfit. Then the penny dropped.

"Oh, St Patrick's Day is it?"

"Yes, all day and I'm determined to celebrate even though I am far from home in a strange land," said the girl cheerily.

"Oh, and what will you be celebrating it with?"

"A Guinness stew, a Guinness drink and the company of workmates."

The girl's voice was soft and warm and only slightly inflected by her Irish brogue. "How can I help you," Mrs Williamson ventured. "Are you collecting for something?"

The girl's face coloured slightly. "Oh dear no. I have been sent here by The Metropolis Mrs Williamson."

Jane Williamson's expression changed instantly to one of anger. Her tone became hostile. "Do you really think I want to see anybody else from that damned newspaper today after what your reporter did?"

"I understand Mrs Williamson. I'll just go if you like. But I am not long in the job and they just sent me to say sorry really."

The older woman's face softened. This girl was just how she would like her own oldest daughter to be, vivacious, slim, sociable and not a morose depressive whose comfort eating and drinking was out of hand.

"Come in, why don't you."

Mary followed her in to the livng room where she had earlier poured her heart out to Jeremy Earnshaw and occupied the same seat as he had.

Mrs Williamson fussed around her, insisted on making tea and serving biscuits. A little bit of cheerful chat was going a long way with her.

Mary was very good at light conversation. "Yes I'm from Northern Ireland, from Belfast actually but east Belfast you know. I had a lovely childhood, knew nothing about all the troubles at all."

But inside she didn't feel right, a bit mixed up. She liked Phil Holmes. He seemed a nice man but why on earth had he dragged her in to this mess? It had seemed a genuine request. "Mary, could you do a bit of PR for the newspaper? Go see this lady. I think one of our reporters has gone too far and she could be a legal. Can you just see what she's thinking and report back?"

She couldn't really disagree but it was disappointing to be used in that way. It wasn't a proper assignment. And yet Holmes was supposed to fancy her. No way to treat a girl you fancy. If Holmes had just asked her out she would have said yes. She loved making new friends and going out. She liked George too. Those steely blue eyes of his. He was so casual, too laid back by far. But those eyes said there was more to him than that. If George asked her out she would say yes but there was no sign of that either. He was such a dreamer. Maybe it was best she didn't get involved with someone who wanted to be a creative writer and not a hack. Creative people could be very demanding and often went off the rails. She liked a relationship to be steady. She felt a pang of guilt about the man she left behind in Belfast, Tom, the football reporter, and his lovely old sports car. He was such fun but she wasn't missing him that much so it couldn't be love.

"Okay, so why am I getting a second visit?" Mrs Williamson demanded as she sat down opposite Mary on a wicker lounge chair.

"I'm not totally sure," Mary said candidly, "but I think my boss just wanted to show you we cared. He was very bothered about you being upset and all and went straight to our editor about it."

"Oh good. Well, I'm sorry but I don't think the conduct of this reporter can be excused. What he did was theft."

"Yes, Mrs Williamson."

"I mean, do you know what he did?"

Mary shook her head.

"He took out a rather large edition of the bible out of his briefcase and said something to the effect that all the answers were within or something. Then he put it back in his briefcase and, on reflection, I think it was at that point that he slipped the photograph inside it."

Mary was stunned. Second week in the job and she had to tell her bosses that their star reporter was a crook. The silence that had fallen between the two women was broken only by the footsteps of the paper boy and the dull thud of his delivery in to the hallway.

Mrs Williamson jumped up to get the paper. Only to be expected when your loved one was going to be the main item in it, Mary thought.

But the scream that came from the hallway wasn't expected at all. Mary leapt up and raced out of the living room to find Mrs Williamson sitting semi-collapsed on the floor.

"They've used it," she screamed. "They've put the photo of my little darling all over the paper for all the world to see. How dare they?"

Mary felt trapped and scared. What did she do if Mrs Williamson fainted. Why was the photo in the paper? Holmes had proudly told her how he got it pulled. She had never had a St Patrick's Day like it.

"They're all the same," screamed Mrs Williamson. "They're all bloody liars just out to get what they want. They don't care who gets hurt."

"I was told they wouldn't use the photo Mrs Williamson," Mary said quietly.

The older woman picked herself up, turned her anger upon her. "Then you've been conned as well young lady. I feel violated."

Mary put a consoling arm around her but it was shrugged off.

"Just get out," Mrs Williamson hissed, "and tell your editor that I will take this further. You can tell him that I am no idiot and I know how these things work."

Mary left quickly, her brain swirling with various emotions but mostly pity for Mrs Williamson and contempt for herself.

Maybe George had a point.

SEVEN

Cowley had patiently waited for his moment from 6.30am when he was first man in to the office, sleepily carrying the huge bundle of morning newspapers he picked up at reception and then throwing them on to the command desk. The crashing noise he made invariably annoyed the cleaners who were just finishing their overnight work.

He waited as the office filled up, waited for his prey. Sharpe was the late man, wandering in anonymously like a man who liked being the last in the queue. Self-effacement seemed a fine art with Sharpe. Cowley had spent a lot of time wondering about the newsroom's enigma boy. He was plumb bottom of his League of Death yet seemed not to have the slightest concern about it.

Sharpe made a beeline for the coffee machine. Cowley looked at his watch. 9am. He should have walked directly over to the command desk for the orders of the day. Not Sharpe. Cowley was tired of reminding him that they were in the business of deadlines.

Sharpe took a couple of sips from his plastic cup and had a good look around the newsroom like a man on his first day in prison, soaking everything up. Slowly, via greetings to colleagues and squints at various newspapers lying around occasional vacant desks, he arrived at the command desk, looking calmly down at the seated Cowley from his 6ft frame.

"Morning."

"Morning George. Nice of you to drop in."

"I'm on time."

"You were on time at the coffee machine as usual."

Sharpe muttered something under his breath. Cowley thought he heard the word jobsworth but decided to let it go.

"What's this I hear about you in a fracas in a little bookstore George?"

Sharpe's expression changed to something similar to a rabbit caught in the headlights of a speeding BMW. "What are you talking about?" he snapped.

"I heard you got thrown out of W.H. Smith's, the one in Grainger Street."

Sharpe's neck started to glow red. Then it spread to his face. He nervously unbuttoned his blazer and felt the knot in his tie.

"It seems a strange time and place to create a scene, mid-afternoon in a bookshop."

"It's a personal thing. I don't suppose you would understand."

"Try me." Cowley moved his arms outward in a bid to encourage his strangest reporter to say more.

"I thought time was of the essence."

Cowley glanced down at his news list. The name Sharpe was neatly typed alongside Mags.

"You're down for court and nothing else at the minute—10am at the city magistrates."

Sharpe sighed: "Not those wankers again, deliberating about human rights for hours on end."

"Now then George, we get some good stories come from court. But come on, I want to hear about this fracas."

Sharpe's stubbly face was slowly returning to its normal paleness. "I just lost my cool with the dickhead manager. It was just words but maybe I shouldn't have shouted so much."

"They marched you out, yes?" Cowley was trying hard not to snigger. Holmes had looked up from his screen as he picked up on the conversation.

"Well, him and his security men. There was no need for it. It was just words."

"But you're a big fellow George. They might have found you intimidating."

"I'm not particularly aggressive, only if I am cornered. I was just making a point."

"And the point was?"

"His window display basically. Full of crappy biographies by fat chefs, loudmouth DJs and football WAGs. I just blew my top."

"Were you shouting something about War and Peace? Tale of Two Cities? Angry Young Men."

Sharpe sighed. "I don't think I was shouting. I was suggesting he put some literature in his front street display window, not fill it with big smiley crap."

"Surely, it's the manager's business to manage how he sees fit."

Sharpe gave Cowley a withering look. "He's dealing in books. Books bring knowledge, enlightenment, the right books anyway. But his display window is just like a mirror for people to look at their ugly selves in. I was just trying to tell him he could do more for his city, more for the people in it. Make them think maybe, instead of trying to cook steakburgers on a griddle pan."

Holmes, who had been listening with interest, did what Cowley had been trying desperately not to do. He burst in to laughter and actually smiled. "I like it. I believe I am looking at a would-be writer."

He turned to Cowley. "Not an everyday hack this one. Give him a bit of rope. We're a broad church in journalism you know."

Cowley was astonished at the reaction of Holmes. More faces were turning from their screens on the command desk to see what the fuss was. Sharpe's voice was getting louder and Cowley glanced nervously round fearing it might bring the editor out of his office.

". . . . instead of buying books knocked out in a day by somebody who won a talent show singing somebody else's song, or somebody who shagged a millionaire footballer."

"Okay, Sharpe. I've heard enough. Time to do some work," Cowley tried to put the lid on Sharpe's rant but couldn't.

"I mean it's a cracked society we live in and it's not going to get any better with people like that running bookshops."

Cowley's frame sagged as he realised the editor was now standing behind his chair. Chalmers' voice cut through the entire office like a cracked whip.

"A cracked society is good, gives us good stories. Now can you buggers write some and stop discussing the state of the nation?"

Cowley nodded his acquiescence and looked back to find a space where Sharpe had been standing.

"Yes boss," he muttered.

Cowley buried his head in the papers on his desk. His neatly typed League of Death was the top one.

Sharpe's name was bottom of the list.

Holmes had ruled the roost in the newsroom for a whole year now and was proud of his record. He had thought of quitting when Chalmers pulled the stroke on him by running the picture of the meningitis girl. But then he thought better. A year was a long time in newspapers. Holmes was busy catching up with old friends on Facebook, updating on where they were and what they were doing. An old boss of his was now an executive on The Daily Mail in Manchester. Fleet Street rates would be nice if he could get them. He would earn as much or maybe more than Chalmers. Holmes was becoming tired of provincial newspapers. The news world was his oyster. Why had he stayed so long in Newcastle? He knew the answer was his attachment to the place where he was born and bred, to his mum and dad in historic Seaton Delaval where he visited every Sunday, to the old school pals he still played five-a-side with and who fed him with stories. But Chalmers' dirty deed over the meningitis girl's pictures had put things in perspective. If he had to work with someone slightly crooked he might as well be in the nationals and not in the in-between land of regionals where cheque book journalism was frowned upon. It was a convenient perspective for managements who didn't want to invest too much money on the editorial section of their newspaper, as was always the case. The faceless boardroom money men wanted investment in advertising staff who paid for their jobs by finding income streams for the paper. He cared about his job and took pride in doing it well. It was important for Holmes to be able to account to his readers. He knew he couldn't do that with Mrs Williamson and he sensed there would be more people like her.

He couldn't do much about Chalmers. Behind the slick façade which his editor presented to his public was a manipulative, bullying force which plundered the vast sea of news like a pirate ship.

But he could do something about Earnshaw, the supreme ego of the newsroom. The 24-year-old who had virtually stalked him since joining The

Metropolis from a weekly newspaper. Earnshaw had been so keen to get on that he seemed to turn up everywhere that Holmes sought relaxation after work.

It had started in the local pub for the city hacks, The Rat. If Holmes called in after work it was guaranteed Earnshaw would drop in soon after and offer to buy drinks. Foolishly, Holmes had confided in Earnshaw the names of the other city pubs he liked, pubs where he could get away from his colleagues and engage with people from other walks of life. Earnshaw had started turning up in these locations, something which could only be achieved, Holmes knew, by following him discreetly. Then Earnshaw had turned up at the gym where Holmes played five-a-side with his old school buddies and Holmes had been unable to take anymore. There was an unpleasant confrontation.

"Look Jeremy,' Holmes told the laser-eyed younger man. "This has got to stop. You will earn my respect by doing your job and nothing else but. I can't stop you going to the places where I enjoy myself but I think you need to find your own."

Earnshaw seemed to accept the rebuke and had stopped intruding on his private spaces. Instead he had ploughed all his energy in to being top dog of the newsroom coldly glaring at Holmes every morning with his eyes of kryptonite until he was given a decent assignment. There was no fobbing him off with a couple of rewrites from the morning newspapers. Homes would play around with them or just forget them if he could find something to get his teeth in to.

So it was in newsrooms; shy bairns got nowt and the dogs who did the most barking got the decent bones. He usually ended up giving the boring crap to Sharpe and getting Earnshaw off his back by sending him out on a job.

But not today. Today was the day of retribution when Earnshaw would learn he had crossed the line in to a dangerous minefield. Holmes had strode over purposefully to where Earnshaw was sitting reading The Sun with his feet up on the desk. "Come on Jeremy, we have to find an empty room for talk talk."

Earnshaw grimaced and threw his paper on to his desk. He rose sloppily from his chair and grabbed his coffee and followed reluctantly. Holmes headed for the small office used by Eddie Black. Black was tied up showing a school group around the building as part of the paper's working with the community programme. Holmes breezed in and took a chair and invited Earnshaw to do likewise.

"I'll not beat about the bush Jeremy. You're in big trouble. I have a lady who has made a serious complaint about you which is basically an allegation of theft. We have to deal with it in the proper way and, if it's true, you could be out of a job."

Holmes had wanted to bring Earnshaw down from his lofty perch and make him squirm. He paused and looked across the desk to study his face but was amazed to see it seemed unperturbed.

"You know what I'm talking about Jeremy?"

Earnshaw met the steely gaze of Holmes with indifference. "Haven't a clue chief. Perhaps you had better hurry up and give uz a clue. I've got fish to fry."

Earnshaw's tone was almost hostile and Holmes suddenly felt an uncharacteristic rush of anger. He prided himself on keeping cool in the worst of situations. He had been able to handle one of the most ruthless editors he had ever worked for and yet this reporter was getting under his skin.

"Mrs Williamson."

"Oh that." A tiny curl of the lips in to almost a grin was the only giveaway from Earnshaw. "So what? It was a good story, yes? I can't help it if the woman's upset about it. She's in grief. People in grief are often confused about things."

Yes, and that's where someone like you takes full advantage, Holmes thought. No sympathy towards the plight of the victim, just another mourner to plunder for story and pictures and then out of her house and out of her life. These were one in a million things and people like you trade on the fact you won't have to answer to your victims again..

"Mrs Williamson says that you took the picture which was used in The Metropolis from the mantelpiece of her living room without her permission. She's not a stupid woman Jeremy. She is taking legal advice and I think you should take this seriously. What have you got to say?"

"What have I got to say," Earnshaw yawned and slowly stretched his arms in boredom. "What I have got to say is this: why am I sitting here being screwed by you when I could be out getting you a good story? You're wasting my time."

"What have you got to say?" Holmes shouted across the desk now so loudly that heads were raised around the editorial floor.

"I asked her if we could use the picture on the mantelpiece and she said yes."

"And what about the bible you got out of your briefcase?" Holmes was still shouting, becoming red in the face.

"Oh, that's just an old trick Phil. I always carry it. It makes a big difference with some people, I can tell you."

Holmes held back his anger and tried to cool down. "It's a distraction trick, something a thief would do. You distracted her attention while you swiped the picture."

Earnshaw's face contorted for the first time but not with contrition. Instead his huge eyes bore in to Holmes's face with projected fury. "Fuck off. I didn't."

"I think you did."

"You can think what you like. At the end of the day it's my word against hers and she's all messed up anyway."

"She wasn't messed up until you got in to her house."

"So you say. What would you know anyway? Sitting at your desk day in day out. You're never out there on the doorstep. You don't know what it's like."

"I used to be. I know how it works."

"Yeah? Well, do what you want It's not going to hurt me."

"I was going to suggest you be given written warnings for starters here but your attitude is so bad I'm going straight in with a recommendation for dismissal."

"Okay, you do that," Earnshaw sneered. "You're not going to screw me. I've already seen Chalmers about it."

"You what!" Holmes couldn't believe the intransigence of Earnshaw.

"Yeah, I bumped in to him in the Collingwood Arms, the pub where all the footballers go. We had a chat. He said great job and don't worry about a thing. He said I was top of the league, you know"

Holmes jerked a thumb towards the door indicating the session was over. He would have to put in a report to Chalmers but Chalmers had already made up his mind.

Earnshaw had proved that his stalking paid.

EIGHT

The conversation was so obtuse that Black was still pondering over it hours later. He had a feeling that something very bad would come out of it.

He had been called in to the office of Gareth Chalmers to find an editor in turmoil, wringing his hands in despair, pointing to crumpled papers on his desk.

"The bastards," he proclaimed as Black strode in to the room.

"What boss?"

"The bastards want to cut jobs," Chalmers said and pointed again at the letters. Black could just make out the words HUMAN RESOURCES in large letters on the sheets.

"Their business plan isn't working for Newcastle, Eddie. We are not making enough profit. That's what they are saying. The Venezuelans are screaming that their money is being spread around like rain with nothing to show for it and that useless bastard Morton is pointing the finger at us. He's a national newspaper man. He doesn't understand regionals. The nationals never do. They take all the stuff we bring them and then they shit on us. They thought they could just ride in to Newcastle and do great business . It was great at first. There was no limit. They poached all the best reporters working for the other lot and it seemed to work but it would appear Joe Public is getting bored with us and the other lot are fighting back. What to do Eddie, what to do?"

"Call a meeting, let's see if anyone wants out. There are one or two oldies who might."

Chalmers eyeballed him. "One or two's no good. I want ten. I want to take it down to the bone then they won't be able to come back next year for more."

Black waited. He had learned to only bounce one suggestion at a time off his boss Two suggestions was an invitation to be hit with channelled anger.

The silence lasted a considerable time then Chalmers looked up at Black and began talking in what seemed to him a conspiratorial tone.

"You know this list that I don't know about?"

"What boss?"

"The list man, Cowley's fucking list that I don't know about."

"Oh, The League of Death." Black's face creased with pleasure at his own powers of recall then froze in sobriety under the withering gaze from Chalmers.

"Yes, the list I know nothing about. Now, have you got that?"

Black coughed. "Yes, I've got that boss. We're talking about The League of Death and I'm the only one in this room that could possibly know about The League of Death and if anyone ever asks me if anyone at a higher level knew about it I will say no. It's safe with me boss. The buck stops here."

Chalmers smiled. "Yes Eddie, this list that I don't know about is our starting point. How many general news reporters are on it?"

"Sixteen now sir."

"Okay. So I want a breakdown of those who are scoring and those who are not. The ones on zero, they're no good to me."

"No boss?"

"No Eddie. You know why?"

Black feigned interest. At that moment he really wanted to know why West Ham had not signed a certain player he liked in the transfer window.

"Because death is our business. It's what sells our papers. It's what keeps us in jobs here in the regions. That and football."

"I love football, boss. I think we could do more in that area."

"Eddie, there's no doing more in terms of staff levels and we can't really make people work any harder. They're clocking ten hours a day on average already. So the sports staff can consider themselves lucky they will be untouched. No more redundancies there Eddie right?"

"Okay boss."

"But the political guy, what's his name, Morrison, he can go, and the health woman, we can get rid of her. It's all crap that we can get done by London mostly, make that bugger in the House of Commons work a bit."

"Yes, Graham Pilkington, he could do more for us," Black agreed.

" But the list, the list I don't know anything about Eddie, is a bloody good measure of which reporters are the key to this title's survival. The zeros are out of the door. Alright?"

Black nodded, inwardly aghast.

"I reckon about half that list should do it. Eight reporters. A couple of specialists and that's it. A nice round 10. That should keep them happy."

"Eight of the general news reporters boss?"

Yes, the bottom half has to go because they are all crap, okay?"

"Okay boss, I'm on the case."

"Okay. So, any ideas for conference?"

"No boss."

"Good man. I like your honesty. I don't like these shit executives who put up ideas just because they think they should. They have to be served up with passion. That's what I like."

"Yes, boss."

Black was rustling papers and heading for the office door.

"Get me a coffee will you Eddie?"

"Yes boss, pronto."

Black could feel that old twitch in his neck starting off, the one that came on when he was being harassed. It was time to be heading down the M1 again.

Jones, Michael James, 50, Gosforth, suddenly as the result of an accident . . . .

The words of Holmes rang in Sharpe's ears as he drove the car through Newcastle's central motorway system and headed for Gosforth. Holmes was possibly the most reasonable of all the people he worked for and he believed what he said: "This could be your last chance George. The editor is pencilling in the names for redundancies and you're in the hat. I could give this to Earnshaw. He would eat it up. But here you go. Try and get out of the relegation zone."

Sharpe would have liked to have said something casual. Something like: "Please yourself, doesn't bother me." But his mortgage and car loan stopped him. Why did he have a mortgage anyway? Damn his three wise men uncles. He dutifully accepted the death notice which had been cut out of the paper and pasted on to sheet of A4 to give it more significance and make it less easy to lose.

Jones. Michael James, 50, Gosforth. Suddenly as the result of an accident. Greatly missed by Jane, Ben and Jill.

Sharpe mused over the names. Ben and Jill sounded like the names of young kids. Jane would be his wife. The realisation of possibly meeting them within the next hour left him feeling cold and sad. What right did he have to disturb their grief-stricken world?

His thoughts were interrupted by an ad jingle on the radio His stand-up comic friend Geoff was playing Newcastle City Hall next week. He would have to go see him.

He recalled more words of advice from Holmes. "Could be a good one. I hear he's a businessman. Road accident in his BMW but looks like he deliberately drove it in to an empty bus."

Sharpe parked his car in a quiet street and made a careful note of the mileage in the back of his notebook. He had decided to use his own car and claim mileage after a run-in with the paper's garage manager on his first week in the job. He had been wrongly accused of damaging a pool car, a common occurrence as the manager tried to cover his tracks following the battering of the cars by photographers in particular. He put his notebook in a side pocket ready for use.

He had the address from a search of the electoral register and the trail led him to a small detached house in affluent Gosforth suburbia with a long drive guarded by black iron gates which were closed and locked. He pressed buttons on an intercom system on the wall beside the gates but got no response. Capulet Grove was a dead end in all senses of the word.

Sharpe stuffed his notebook back inside his coat. There was nothing else he could do. He was contemplating on whether to telephone Holmes or just head back when a voice broke in to his thoughts. "Can I help you, young man?"

Sharpe turned to find a middle-aged, white-faced woman standing with handbag and serious inquiring gaze, Margaret Thatcher style. "Maybe. Do you know the family living here?"

The woman bristled, throwing back her shoulders. "And why might you be asking such a question?"

Sharpe smiled as he fished in a pocket for an ID card. He handed it to the woman. "That's me and that's who I work for."

"Oh, a reporter for The Metropolis," the woman's voice trailed a little as she absorbed all the information on the card. It seemed to go down alright. "The newspapers again."

"Again?'

"Yes, again. He had lost his way and was being hounded. Business worries and the press on his back. Tragic really. His wife had gone back to her mother's with the children. He had appeared in court for drink driving. So sad for a man of science."

"A man of science?"

"Yes. He was the man behind Scientific Solutions."

"Jesus." Sharpe was stunned but quickly recovered his composure. "Sorry about that word. I just got a shock myself."

The woman had appeared offended by his language but accepted his apology. "Well it is such a shock. He was so successful."

Sharpe suddenly felt a peculiar feeling in his body. It was excitement. He knew he was on the trail of the late Jim Jones, a man who had just become a millionaire with the floating of his company on the stock market, a man whose photograph was already in the newspaper library as a result of his court appearance for drink driving, which made Sharpe's job for today much easier, a man who had courted controversy with his public stand that euthanasia was both acceptable and necessary and had pledged his company to its goal.

"You say his family left him. Do you know where I might find them?"

"Well, down London young man but I have no idea of the address. Samantha's father was a barrister and they were very close. He would have had no hesitation in taking her back when the marriage started to fail. She was a lovely woman. She couldn't stand anymore of her husband's ways."

"Samantha? Who is Jane and Ben and Jill?"

"That will be his sister and her children."

She stopped talking for a moment and Sharpe waited, remembering the advice of Tony Carver. "Sometimes silence is the best interviewer of all. Once a person wants to talk they will usually tell you nearly everything they know."

He listened as the woman told him about the rumours sweeping the neighbourhood. The word was that Jones had not been able to handle the pressure of the onslaught he had faced for advocating euthanasia. A young and bright scientist who believed in free speech and the freedom of ideas, he had not anticipated the world's press being camped on his doorstep for days on end, the interest of the Northumbria police force in his statement which had to be referred to the Director of Public Prosecutions for possible criminality. He had started to behave strangely. His wife had taken the kids down to London to live with her dad.

Sharpe listened and tried to lock as much away as possible in his head of what the woman was saying. He had again remembered Carver's advice about notebooks. "Sometimes it's like pulling out a gun. It scares your punter off. Sometimes it pays to just listen."

He waited until the woman paused again and this time he spoke. "Was there anyone, a friend, someone around here we could speak to, someone who knew Mr Jones?"

"Hah," the woman threw back her head and then pointed it in the direction of a building at the bottom of the street. "You'll find her down in the flats there. She's the only friend he had, if you can call it that, if you can call a hooker a friend."

"A hooker, in Capulet Grove, Gosforth?" Sharpe couldn't help smiling. "Please, I'm not being disrespectful but I find that hard to believe.'

"And you a reporter. Don't you know about these nice young girls selling their bodies because they are desperate for money? It's the only way they can pay their bills. She's at university so she needs the money."

"What's her name?"

"Felicity, would you believe?" the woman answered quizzically.

"Ah yes, happiness," Sharpe smiled. "Can I ask your name please?"

"Most certainly not. I don't want my name all over the papers," she snapped back.

Carver had been so right about not always producing your notebook immediately. She would go down as a woman, who refused to be named, when he quoted her in the paper tonight. He said a hasty goodbye and, once out of sight of the woman, began scribbling down everything she had said in to his notebook. Once he had completed the task he headed down towards the flats where Felicity lived. Again his passage was blocked by black iron gates on to a driveway. Again he was faced with an intercom box this time with more than a dozen numbers. He pressed number one, no answer.

He worked his way through to number six without any luck then at last on number seven a female voice answered sounding as if he had woken her up. She sounded young and he hoped it might be Felicity herself.

"Who is it?"

Sharpe explained his mission and thought he could hear faint giggling from the woman.

"You want Felicity, hah, hah. You'll have a hard job. She's like a ship that passes in the night. You never know when she's coming in, when she's leaving. I think she spends a lot of time at the university. And then she has her outside interests, you know."

"Yes, I have heard about that. Are you a friend?"

The woman's tone changed immediately, as if he had accused her of being promiscuous. "Good God, no. I'm a mother-of-two. Look I think I have helped you as much as I can. Is there anything else?"

"Could you just tell me what she looks like?"

"Oh you people. You're looking for a tall blonde, pretty. She seems to wear a long red coat all the time at the moment."

"What's her flat number."

"Nine, now I have told you enough. Thank you and goodbye."

The line went dead. Sharpe thought of ringing her again but then decided she had been so helpful that he should leave her in peace until maybe another time. His mobile cut annoyingly in to his thoughts with a strident electronic jingle. It was Holmes wanting an update. He told him everything that had happened at the home of Jim Jones. Holmes was pleased. There was enough there for today. He would get head office reporters to dig up all the cuttings on Jones. But Holmes was never satisfied with today.

"You might have just saved your job. What about tomorrow? Can you get something for tomorrow?"

"The trail's gone dead but I have a suggestion. Let me take the rest of the afternoon off and I'll have a sniff around tonight. There might be more chance of finding people."

He could almost hear the ticking of Holmes' brain as he weighed up whether to pull Sharpe back in to the office to tap out dross on his keyboard or leave him with freedom of operation.

"Do you think you will get something?'

"Yes, I just think yes."

"Okay."

Sharpe switched off his phone and headed back towards his car. He should have told Holmes about Felicity but why give him the chance to assign other reporters to finding her. He knew it was his lucky break and he was going to make sure it stayed that way.

NINE

Tony Carver had got in to the office a few minutes earlier than usual all pumped up for a big catch. A police chief was due to make his first appearance in the city magistrates' court on a drink driving charge. Carver had watched it from the start when one of the police moles he had cultivated had tipped him off. Rather than run a story about his arrest and tip off radio, tv, and the national newspapers, he had kept it to himself and waited for the first appearance in court of the chief superintendent.

He had stayed fresh by spending the evening mugging up on his multimedia notes. This had kept him out of the pub. In the past, Carver would have walked out on strike with his fellow hacks if he had been told to take pictures. That was a photographer's job. Not anymore. Taking of pictures and videos was now expected of him and he was sent twice a month on courses to explain how it was done. He thought wistfully of the photographers' darkroom of the old days and red roadside telephone boxes as he carefully went through the notes on how to email a picture to the news desk while out on assignment. It used to be nice to go out on the job with a photographer, a time to share a good rant about everything that was wrong with the paper. That was all gone.

He arrived in the office in a state of eager anticipation of hitting the front pages. It was a feeling only a newspaperman can understand, the achievement of being top dog in a den of dogs.

At that time of morning Holmes was in his usual transfixed state of study, poring over a mound of newspapers of all descriptions, weeklies, local daily papers, big regional ones, national tabloids and broadsheets. He always looked resentful at being pulled away from them. You had to have something good to tell him and Carver basked quietly in the knowledge that he was armed with a rocket launcher of a story.

"Good one in court today," he announced casually, "You remember the police chief from Newcastle who got promoted to head the Cumbria force."

"Yes, Walter Ord," Holmes looked uninterested, even agitated.

"Ah well. Here's the thing. Before he left the city he went out with his workmates for a bit of a night out. He got so drunk he decided to drive home in his Mercedes and wrapped it around a lamppost. He was breathalysed by one of the lads he had been out with who had gone straight back on shift."

Holmes managed a mysterious half-grin. It struck Carver that he knew more than he was letting on. He tried to big the story up.

"He was about four times the limit. He's finished as a police officer. He's due in court today so we can snatch a pic and do the business. I mean, c'mon Holmes, this is top of the list stuff."

Holmes blinked and looked Carver directly in the eyes. His look was almost sympathetic.

"Well it is, but why all the excitement Tony? Have you not seen the list."

Holmes was holding up a sheet of A4 with the stories of the day printed on it in bold capitals. Top of the list was POLICE CHIEF'S DAY OF SHAME.

Carver felt his heart start racing. He looked for the name of the reporter alongside the story. It was Earnshaw.

"No way," he muttered.

Holmes put the sheet down and moved his eyes back towards his newspapers, a signal that he wanted Carver to move off and get working on something else. Carver didn't move.

"That's theft,'" he exclaimed loudly. "That's straight bloody theft."

Heads were turning in the newsroom. Holmes was glaring impatiently at him from behind his huge spectacles.

"I'm sorry Phil. Look, I know you have a million and one things on but I have been watching that story for weeks. I had a tip-off from a good contact. You know how good my police contacts are. Earnshaw hasn't got police contacts. They don't trust him."

Holmes shrugged. "Believe me Tony, there is no one who wants rid of Earnshaw more than me at the moment. But he seems to be the early bird with the worm on this one. He came in very early. I have never seen him in the office before me before. I daresay he is trying a bit of damage limitation. He has got to be a bit worried at the moment. He's being monitored, you know, after this business with the meningitis kid's picture."

Carver recognised he was beaten and marched back towards his desk. As he went to sit down he caught his leg on a drawer.

"Shit," he exclaimed and was again the source of stares around the newsroom.

He looked down at the open drawer and realised how he had been scooped by Jeremy Earnshaw.

"Someone's broken in to my desk," he yelled. He picked up the broken lock that was lying on the floor and stood up shouting across the newsroom to Holmes.

"Someone has broken the lock on my desk. I have been burgled. My diary has gone."

Holmes appeared to be ignoring Carver. He was looking directly up at the ceiling of the office, at a small cctv camera trained on the area below. He was smiling broadly.

Earnshaw was wound up like a spring. He had been sitting in court for a good two hours listening to magistrates waffling on about a human rights issue in a case of shoplifting. The courtroom clock told him he had half an hour to first edition.

He felt uneasy. His hands were aching. There were unused to being asked to perform feats of physical strength and forcing the padlock on Carver's desk with some small bolt croppers had taken some strength.

His mind was racing because he had actually done something very naughty. Normally he would not have worried at all but there was already the meningitis kid thing that was on the go. Chalmers was okay but Phil Holmes was after him big style. They had been talking about giving him a written warning.

He looked almost pleadingly at Norman Johnson, an ex-miner who was the lead magistrate on the bench of three. He was sitting just four metres away from the press box in an elevated podium with one fellow magistrate on each side of him. Johnson looked back blankly. The shoplifter was dealt with and there was a lull in proceedings while the court usher tried to find the next defendant.

Johnson's curiosity got the better of him. "What brings the gentlemen of the press to the court today then?" he inquired magisterially from on high.

"Case number 61 your worships, Walter Ord," Earnshaw replied crisply.

Johnson's big round face made a sweep of the court until it pinpointed the prosecuting solicitor.

"Can we help the gentleman of the press Mr Dyson. Can we bring on this Walter Ord before the court?"

Austin Dyson tried to mask his contempt for the press with a measured response. "He is in the queue your worships, shouldn't be too long."

Johnson's face swept back to Earnshaw. "Well there you are. I have tried. I can't hurry Mr Dyson."

Dyson turned his back to the bench and aimed a hostile stare at Earnshaw. Just as he did the swing doors in to the court flew open and two men marched in. Earnshaw looked across to see one of them was Carver who looked enraged. He glared at Earnshaw and held up a fist towards him.

The other man walked up to the magistrates and spoke to Johnson whose face suddenly became serious. He gave a nod of consent and the other man marched over to Earnshaw.

"Jeremy Earnshaw, I need you to come with me."

"But I'm working. I'm reporting a case. You're trying to gag the press," he blurted.

"I think the press is going to be represented by Mr Carver here while I speak to you about a little matter. I don't want to embarrass you Mr Earnshaw so just come along."

"Who are you?"

"Det Insp Johnson, of City CID."

Earnshaw choked back tears as he slid out from behind the shelter of the press box and followed the police officer.

Tony Carver had salvaged professionalism from a day of stress and strain. His story about the drunken police chief was splashed all over the front of The Metropolis. The silly young news desk number two, Cowley, was running around pointing out Carver's name at the top of his stupid League of Death. Carver had made it clear from the start that he wanted nothing to do with the league. He had told Holmes so in no uncertain terms. However, it did feel good to have foiled Earnshaw's attempt to hijack top place. No-one could have known that Carver was enjoying the demise of Earnshaw as he sat engrossed with his screen and keyboard, paying no attention to anyone else around him. But he never missed a trick.

The newsroom would be so much better off without Earnshaw and now maybe Sharpe and the Irish girl, Mary, could get a bit of the action. They were good sorts and there was no reason why nice people couldn't do a good professional job. Too many of the younger reporters quickly slipped in to a hardnosed stereotype of how they thought a reporter should be, quickly slipped in to each other's beds as well. He got tired of watching the casual sex which went on in the office. Kirsty, in particular, seemed to be using seduction as her career shaper.

He had no hesitation in urging Holmes to call in the police and Holmes had wasted no time in finding videotape evidence of Earnshaw's crime. It wasn't the first time Earnshaw had stolen material from him. Carver had marked his card after the Premiership footballer sex scandal. Carver had met a kiss and tell wannabe when he allowed himself to be persuaded to go to see Bon Jovi at the Newcastle Arena with another hack. She had cottoned on to him being a reporter and told him of her relationship with the married striker. He had offered to advise her on how to get the best deal out of the nationals while making sure the story hit The Metropolis as well, the best a regional man could do faced with the spending power of the nationals. He had put a date in his diary and a telephone number to get her in a week or so On a day off he had picked up his paper from the corner shop to see Earnshaw's byline splashed alongside a picture of the starry-eyed wannabe.

When an indignant Carver took his diary to Holmes and complained of treachery in the camp Earnshaw fished out his own diary to show his own neat entries in the appropriate dates. Neither Holmes or Carver were fooled but nothing could be done. "You'll have to keep your diary on you," was all Holmes said, "Get one of those little pocket ones."

Carver had kept his diary under lock and key from that date on. People like Earnshaw just knew no limits. Like the phone hackers who had caused so much trouble in the industry, they were a danger to the profession.

Pentleton, Amy, Newcastle, three months, died tragically . . . .

The ruins of Llactapata and Sayaqmarka, the lost city of Machu Picchu. The exotic Inca Trail of Peru was calling. Kirsty Cunningham had been putting away at least £50 a week towards her adventure of a lifetime for a year now and was ready to buy the flight tickets. It was now more important to her than ever that she got away from the reality of life as a reporter on The Metropolis, especially after the day she had just endured.

"This one needs a woman's touch," Cowley said as he handed her the death notice. "A young baby, a young mum, what more can I say? Good heartbreaker if you can get it with pictures and all, even a bit of video for the website would be nice."

She had tried to look appreciative. She was being given an important job. But the idea of the knock gave her butterflies in her stomach. She had gone dutifully out on the job, locating the mum in a sprawling estate on an industrial new town near Newcastle. The house was full of neighbours and relatives wanting to help the family in their grief. She was welcomed and accepted without any questions and found herself in a small living room with a number of toddlers and babies playing with toys and playbooks on the carpet while the adults sipped tea and talked in soft, respectful tones.

Kirsty knew she had to make a statement quickly before she could be accused of getting in to the house on false pretences. She declined an offer to take a chair at the dining table, the only vacant seat in the room, and tried to strike a serious but sympathetic note.

"I just need to tell you all that I am here as a representative of The Metropolis newspaper. The editor felt we should call to express our sympathies and see if there is anything we can do to help, if the family might want to share its loss with our readers. I am sorry to have to call at a time like this but it is something we are expected to do as journalists."

A tense silence fell upon the room and Kirsty felt her stomach knotting again. A woman sitting at the dining table tutted and said: "Well I never." Her husband patted her arm.

The eyes of all the adults in the room drifted from Kirsty to a young woman in a dressing gown playing with the children near a bay window which was strewn with condolence cards.

"What do you want to do?" the woman asked with a trace of a half-smile.

"Are you the baby's mum," Kirsty asked softly.

"Yes, I'm Tracey. Tracey Pentleton," she offered.

"Would you like to talk about the baby and what happened? Our readers would be interested to know about it."

Another half a smile and a nod from Tracey. Noone else said a word and nobody budged from their seats. The kids were getting restless with their playtime. It was going to be a difficult interview.

Kirsty had done several death knocks for The Metropolis and thought she was getting quite professional in her manner. You gently got all the facts. You got some nice quotes. You got pictures. You got out.

"Can you tell me a little bit about your baby maybe what she was like?" It seemed a daft question. All babies seemed the same to Kirsty but you had to tread patiently to get to the nub of the story.

"She was lovely," Tracey gushed. She was a pretty baby-faced woman, still a little chubby from birth and breast feeding and looking tired and worn in her dressing gown. "She was my fourth. I have three little boys. Melanie was my first daughter. She was so pretty and smiley already."

"She got that off her mum," a man on a sofa said and there were sighs of sympathy around the room. The tension seemed to be easing a little and Kirsty asked the names of the boys. Tracey pointed them out as they played on the floor. "James, John and George."

"Names of kings," a voice said and there were more sighs of sympathy.

"And how long had you been married?" Kirsty asked.

"I'm not married. That just didn't work for me. Single mum and proud of it."

The tension seemed to be back in the room. Kirsty looked at the boys again wondering if they all had the same father. She had come across a few single mum families in this part of the world as part of her job. It seemed almost a cottage industry. It was time to wrap this one up.

"Can you tell me what happened Tracey, how Melanie died?"

"A rubber," Tracey welled up in tears fighting for her words. She was on her mat and the boys were drawing. It was all in a split second. She somehow got hold of a rubber and put it in her mouth. She choked. There was nothing we could do, nothing the paramedics could do."

"She should never have been near it," a voice said bitterly from the corner of the room. "She should never have been able to get hold of it."

It came from a small, middle-aged woman sitting on a chair next to one of the sofas, a relation from the paternal side maybe. Kirsty closed her notebook.

"Can we maybe go in to another room or something?" she asked but it was to no avail. A general hubbub had broken out amongst the relatives with voices getting higher and accusations flying. Tracey was right in the middle of it. Kirsty got out with only half the story to take with her. Everybody was too busy shouting to pay her any attention. As she was leaving she made a note of the telephone number on the handset in the hallway. She could ring Tracey later to sort out the pictures.

Back in the warm security of her small city flat Kirsty followed a virtual Inca trail on her laptop. The experience of the day had put her off motherhood for life. What a responsibility! One small mistake and you have a tragedy and warring relatives on your hands.

No, maybe she might change later. But right now she wanted more than anything to travel and motherhood was so restrictive. She had a few places to see first. Maybe when she hit 30 she might review the situation. That was a few years yet.

And she could do without the stress of news reporting. What else did she have to do to get a job in sports reporting? She had slept with Holmes and two of the sports reporters but still the sports desk would not give her a break.

Truth was, it wasn't so much sport that attracted her as sportsmen. She had slept with most of the football and basketball teams when at university and had become addicted to sex with muscular sportsmen.

When Kirsty tried to count how many men she had slept with since losing her virginity at 15 she became arithmetically challenged.

Still, no good looking backward. Might as well look forward to her next conquest. But motherhood, no way!

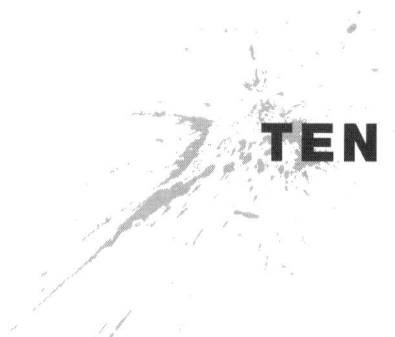

TEN

The awards ceremony to mark the finest in the world of journalism in Newcastle was always staged annually in the city's Civic Centre, a dignified building opened by a Norwegian king in the 1960s, grade ll listed and considered to be a modern classic of its time.

The nine huge flambeaux spanning its entrance had been lit and the bells of the carillon rang to mark the start of the event as Sharpe shuffled in beside Mary Rainwell who had asked him to go with her. Sharpe had not wanted to go. He knew there was no way he had done enough to merit any recognition in the awards but Mary had persuaded him it would be a nice thing to be there.

Having gone against his better instincts in going along with her, Sharpe was left speechless when she abandoned him only minutes after they had joined a dozen other journalists at one of the many long tables straddling the banqueting hall.

"Ah, you know George, I'm sorry but I think I need to do a bit of circulating here. It might not do you any harm to do a bit yourself. Catch you later."

She headed off towards a table nearer to the front of the hall where the prizes would be handed out and sat down next to Phil Holmes who looked delighted to see her. Sharpe couldn't believe the way this left him feeling. He was angry, yes, at being left by her, but also he felt just a pang of jealousy. He did not think he was romantically inclined towards Mary so why this sensation?

Tony Carver, who was sitting next to him, seemed to be reading his mind. " A will-o'-the-wisp, that one son. I would watch you don't get taken for a ride."

Sharpe tried to look unconcerned but couldn't help watching the head-bobbing camaraderie which seemed to have broken out four tables away between Mary and Holmes.

"That's a bit harsh Tony. Why do you say that?"

Carver took a long swig of his pint of Guinness. He loved his ale and was always ready to down a few after work. He was famous amongst journalists for his peculiar trick of being able to drink a pint of beer while holding the glass in his mouth and unaided by hands. It was a rare act and always performed only after a fairly long drinking session. Sharpe had never seen it done but had heard about it.

"One, she's Irish. Two, she's ambitious and three, she's a female reporter. I tell you George in newspapers there is no one more deadly than the female of the species."

Just then the master of ceremonies for the evening, a northern television presenter, announced the first award, for regional news story of the year, and Carver popped up from the table like a spring. Sharpe was amazed at the speed of his movement for so large a man. Two minutes later he was back clutching a small silvery trophy.

"Well, I'd rather have a salary increase," he said, "but hey ho it's a night out."

The next award, for news campaign of the year, went to Phil Holmes, who had led an environmental campaign to clean up the city. Sharpe watched as Holmes returned to his table clutching a similar size trophy to Carver's and was planted with a kiss by Mary.

"That Holmes is a good newsman," said Carver, "but he's got a bit of a weakness for women and it seems to be returned. He's no Brad Pitt either, more a Joe 90, but I tell you every year at these awards he pays for a room in the Station Hotel rather than go home afterwards and every year a different woman goes back with him. I think it was Kirsty last year. Then he goes back to his wife and kids next day."

The night dragged on for Sharpe. The Metropolis won a total of six awards to end up equal on the count with The Sentinel journalists. Carver never stopped talking and, as he got drunker, started confiding in him.

"We've got a bad editor George. Chalmers is a crackhead. That's why he is always so pumped up. He'll burn out, you mark my words. He can't be trusted to do us rank and file journalists any good, too busy chasing women. Holmes is a good man. He misbehaves discreetly. He's always on top of his job, future national editor, no bother. Keep on his right side, you will be ok."

By 10 o'clock the banqueting hall was like a dinner on the eve of battle. There were empty champagne bottles on every table. Fighting was breaking out between reporters and photographers.

Sharpe was in the toilets feeling uselessly sober when he decided to bail out and do something. He had a worried feeling that Carver, now drunk and talking endlessly, was about to show off his pint drinking trick and didn't want to be around in case the glass broke. He tried to attract as little attention as possible as he sidled out of the gents and headed for the cloakroom kiosk at the entrance. The attendant gave him his coat and he was nearly out of the building when he heard the voice of Mary Rainwell.

"Just where do you think you are going?"

Sharpe felt like giving her a mouthful but tried to stay cool. "What's it to you Mary? You seem to be enjoying yourself well enough."

She strode over to him and put her arm through his. "Wherever you're going I'm going wit you. Get me out of here Sharpe. Tee hee. That works both ways. It's your name and it also means get me out of here quick."

She was giggly with drink and very likeable with it but Sharpe wasn't moved. "You don't want to leave now surely."

"I do and don't call me Shirley. I need to get out of here George. That bloody Holmes, he thinks he's Brad Pitt. He wants to take me back to his hotel room and ravish me and I'm not up for it in any way whatsoever. Get me out of here."

"Come on then. Actually I'm going to call on a good time girl and your company would be welcome."

"No, second thoughts, I'm not having three in a bed either. I'm not that sort of girl."

"I know that Mary. I'll explain in the car. It's all in the line of duty. We both need to make our mark."

"You're telling me. I've got it from the horse's mouth. You and I are for the bullet, bottom of the list. We are in the relegation zone buddy. But if I sleep with Mr Phil Holmes tonight he will ride to the rescue wearing his superhacko vest."

The pair headed for his car arm in arm, George having to prop Mary a little to get her there.

They were in Capulet Grove by 10.30. The intercom box looked even less welcoming in the darkness but at least he had a number to press, number nine. A voice answered straightaway.

"Hi, is that Felicity?" he asked quietly and calmly.

"Yes it is. Who speaks?" Her voice was pleasant and relaxed.

"George Sharpe."

"Ah very nice Mr Sharpe. Can you just stand in line with the little camera there and I can see what you look like."

Sharpe repositioned himself so that he was picked up by the tiny lens above the flat numbers. It struck him that Felicity was probably pretty used to dealing with strangers at all times of the day and night and he maybe didn't need to apologise for the late hour of call.

"Okay, what can I do for you?"

"Just a minute. There's someone with me. Her name is Mary Rainwell."

He motioned Mary to stand in front of the lens.

"Yes, very good. I'm intrigued. You had better explain what you want."

"Well, we are both reporters. We work for The Metropolis."

"I'm one of your readers. I get it delivered. It's a good read. Can you show me your ID cards?"

Sharpe had already learned, despite his short span of time in journalism, that there were two kinds of people in the world, those that wanted to talk to newspapers and those who didn't. This girl was definitely in the former camp. On checking their cards through the lens she opened the gates without even asking why they wanted to see her.

The pair walked slowly up the drive, Mary was silent. He had asked her to be an observer and record the interview in her notebook without asking questions. At the entrance to the apartments block they were buzzed in by Felicity. They took a lift to the third floor and found the door at number 9 open for them.

Felicity waved them both towards a big sofa in her bright living room which was minimal in ornaments and had a 52 inch television as a centrepiece. There were no carpets or radiators just a wooden tiled floor with underfloor heating. She was slim, with long black hair and casually dressed in jeans and T shirt. She had the appearance of a university student who enjoyed the support of a rich family.

"I think I know what you want to talk about. My neighbour spoke to a reporter who was snooping around yesterday. Would you like some tea before we start?"

The two reporters waited silently as Felicity rustled around in the kitchen. Sharpe was weighing up his first question. He decided it should be a casual start.

"Okay. So you know we want to speak to you about Mr Jones. We are trying to put together a picture of him for the paper so if you could tell us what he was like."

Felicity smiled and sat down on a chair opposite her interrogators calmly sipping her tea. "He was nice enough with me but there was a lot going on with him, a lot of anger inside."

"Anger at what."

"You lot and the police basically. Scientific Solutions was about a lot more than euthanasia but because Jim took it on as a scientific problem and said what he thought was the solution he became hounded by the press and the police. And he was an up and downer you know. He would be all fired up one day about some great thing he had achieved and then all down the next about some little thing that had upset him. I didn't think he would take his own life. I wished he had come to me about it."

"How often did you used to see him?"

"A lot, after his wife and kids left their home. I don't know why she left him. It was before all the euthanasia fuss. He said she had a fling with another man and he was willing to get over it but she had changed, been consumed by this affair, and couldn't share her bed with him again. It must have been very bad for him."

"So he came to you for friendship."

The hint of a smile never left Felicity's face as she talked and now it broadened in to a grin. "He came to me for friendship and for love and passion and I gave him all three. I was a little bit in love with him myself."

Sharpe was distracted by Mary Rainwell who had started tapping her right foot on the tiled floor. She had her head down on her notebook as she wrote but he could see her cheeks were bright red.

He turned back to Felicity. "It's not for me to judge," he said, "but I have to mention this. Your neighbour says you are a hooker."

"She did, did she?" the smile left her face momentarily and Sharpe feared his interview was at stake. She took a sip of her tea and her smile returned.

"Mrs White always has to put thinks in such stark terms. I'm not a sleazy streetwalker. I don't hang around alleyways bathed in red lights. I work for a high class escort agency, High Heels, and I actually think I provide a useful service."

"But you take payment for having sex with strangers, yes?" Mary's voice cut in to their conversation like a knife.

Sharpe glared at her and looked back to see Felicity sipping tea again. She sighed before answering Mary's question.

"Yes, that's true, very high payments for a very specialised service. You wouldn't believe some of the people I meet, premiership footballers, pilots, lawyers. It became very social after I started going to the mansion house. I would just meet people there that I liked and they would know I was a professional who could give them a service."

"The mansion house?"

"Yes, it's a big house set on an acre in a backstreet in Gosforth. The word was that it belonged to a Crown Court judge although I never got to meet any judges. But there were lawyers, TV presenters, local celebrities and well known faces. You would be surprised."

"Name some names," Sharpe dared her.

"Not a chance. I don't want to jeopardise my income. And, on the subject of names, you won't be putting mine in the paper will you?"

Mary had snapped shut her notebook making a loud noise in the process. Sharpe looked across to see her face was a mask of anger. He fished in his pocket for the car keys and passed them to her. "Oh, yes. You have someone to see at the Civic Centre don't you?" was all he could think of saying.

He was grateful that she said no more and left him with Felicity.

"I'm sorry, I think my friend is a staunch Catholic."

"Well, that's a cross she will have to bear then. Maybe you as well. I think you like her."

"She's just a friend."

"About names George and what are you doing with this interview?"

"Okay. I can refer to you as a friend of Mr Jones who wanted to remain nameless when I write the story. No indication of where you live or anything like that."

"No, I'm happy to talk to you and you can ring me anytime as long as I stay anonymous. And I don't want any pictures, silhouettes or doctored photos of me or anything like that."

"You seem to know a lot about how we work."

"Of course. I'm doing media studies at the city university. We've just been doing the journalist's code of conduct, you know the one that ensures you protect the identity of sources who supply information in confidence and material gathered in the course of her or his work."

"I'm impressed." He was more than impressed. He was amazed but he tried to move forward.

"Do you have any pictures of Jim Jones?"

"Ah, yes. You will love it."

She disappeared and came back with a large A4 envelope which she had sealed.

"Can that be all for tonight George? I need my beauty sleep."

"Yes, by all means. I can just let myself out."

"There's a button at the entrance door. You just press to let yourself out. Same with the gates. Hope your sweetheart found her way alright."

He gave her one of his calling cards and left.

Back in the car Mary was fuming. "That strumpet of a woman can afford to live like a princess on immoral earnings. It's disgusting."

"Why's it always the woman that's immoral Mary? What about all the men who use her services?"

"They are just bastards."

He didn't tell her what Felicity was studying.

ELEVEN

Holmes had shared his hotel room with Kirsty for the second year running but had spent the night thinking about Mary Rainwell. Now he was wracked by guilty feelings towards his family as he tried to pull a newslist together and nurse a hangover. As he shuffled his papers around in the office, he became aware of a figure at his side.

"Hello George. You're nice and early. What is it?"

Sharpe was beaming. "I'm trying to save my future Phil, and Mary's. I think this should get me up the pecking order."

Felicity had given him an envelope full of pictures but he had decided to show Holmes just the one. It was of a man in whites and sandals standing on a Portuguese quayside in front of a silver ocean going yacht with a 30ft mast.

"Who's this?"

"Jim Jones. The death knock you sent me out on the other day. He bought that yacht last year in Gibraltar."

Holmes' gaze cracked in to a wide smile. "What a great follow-up. You'll make the splash for the second day running You got some good words?"

"Too right I have. I need a joint byline. Me and Mary. She helped me track this down."

"Well get to it. Let's serve it up. Keep Chalmers off our backs. I had a heavy night."

"So I gather."

Holmes looked quizzically at him. "Where did you get to with Mary? I was planning to bed her then Carver tells me she went off with you."

Sharpe smiled. "Yes, we had fun." He disappeared towards his screen to tap the story out leaving a puzzled Holmes staring after him.

"Morning Phil, did I just hear you mention my name?"

Holmes swivelled around to see his editor. Chalmers never came in the office this early. It was always much later, around 9am, just in time for conference.

"I was just saying you would like this one Gareth." He showed him the picture that Sharpe had given him.

"The new lad over there has got a belter of a story for us. Might be this month's champagne prize."

Chalmers frowned and nodded towards his office. "I need to see you in there Phil right now. It's not good I'm afraid."

Holmes dutifully followed his editor in to his office.

Chalmers pointed him to a seat. "There's no point beating about the bush. I might as well tell you now so you can get the ball rolling. The board wants your department slashed by half."

Holmes stiffened in shock. "By half, just like that. Christ, we are stretched enough as it is. We are running on a shoestring."

"That's what they want and, unless you can just swan off out of here and forget about your mortgage, that's what you will have to produce."

Chalmers' tone had become threatening. Holmes stared at the names on the newslist he still carried in his hand. "Okay, so how many general news reporters, how many sports reporters, sub-editors?"

"It's nearly all news reporters Phil. Eight reporters and a couple of other fringe journalists. The rest all stay in place. They are right down to the bone."

"Oh, the way they think." Holmes had put a hand to his brow in despair.

Chalmers gave him a withering look. "The way they think?"

"Yes, the top management, the way they think, I'm bloody sick of it." Chalmers took a step back from his table. Holmes had never raised his voice to him before and was now shouting. "It's always the same. They cut the journalists first and then complain when the circulation falls. Well, as far as I am concerned, hard news reporters do the most important job of all, bringing in the stories that sell newspaper. Carver's story about the soldier put 5,000 on the sales. Sharpe's story today will do the same. Who else does that on a daily basis? Not the sports guys. Least of all, the subs."

"Sharpe's one of the guys to go Phil. All the bottom feeders on that list, that thing that Cowley dreamed up, have to go. Eight of them should do it. That should keep the board quiet."

"You're standing there threatening to cut my department by a half and you expect me to play along. Well, I'm not. I'm going to call a meeting of my staff and, you know what, I'm going to suggest we make some sort of protest. I've had enough."

"Well, it's your mortgage," was all Chalmers would say.

TWELVE

Holmes called a meeting of all the general news reporters as soon as he got out of Chalmers' office. He was boiling mad at the fact that the stupid league of death devised by his number 2 would be the litmus test for who stayed and who went. He took over one of the conference rooms and laid it on the line to his staff. Earnshaw sat at the back, a crumpled figure. The sight of him made Holmes feel good. He was on police bail, innocent until proven guilty, but his days on The Metropolis were numbered now.

"Look, what I have to impress on you all, is the sheer unfairness of what the management wants to do. They want to cut reporters' jobs and nobody else's, no sub-editors, no photographers, no executives. I want to know what you feel about that and what you are prepared to do about it."

Carver made some dignified points about the management's attitude to general news reporters which was, as far as he was concerned, was that they were expendable.

Sharpe chipped in: "Don't you all see? You have nothing to lose but your chains. You don't get treated with respect by a bully until you hit him and hit him hard. We need to hit this bullying management."

"That's a bit simplistic but it's possibly right," said Holmes. "We are being forced in to a position where, if we don't stand up for ourselves, our working lives will become intolerable."

"So why doesn't the union do something here?" The question was from Mary Rainwell.

Holmes gave her a half smile. "Ah, the union, the trade union that has done nothing in Newcastle for years. Every year it says yes to a cost of living increase from the management and that's it. It has no fight in it. It also wants to represent everybody all the time, sub-editors, photographers. There are clear divisions of labour in newspapers. The subs don't want anything to do with reporters. They like to look down on them. In fact, they hate them. They would vote against any kind of protest. They would be too worried about their mortgages. The photographers always go their own way and try to make extra money unofficially on the side. I think the situation here is very specific. It's up to the general news reporters to stand up for themselves."

"And you would back them Phil?" Carver asked.

"Yes, I would walk out with you because what good am I if they take half my staff from me?"

"In that case," said Carver, "I think we are maybe in a stronger position than anyone might think. If we walk out now before they have a chance to make any contingency plans it will hit the content of the paper straightaway. Let's show them just how useless they are without us."

"Someone has to make the call," said Sharpe. "Someone has to lead us out."

"I think that should be me," said Holmes. "But I think that first I have to go back to them and give them one last chance to change their minds."

"Shall we just have a vote on a walkout to be called by Phil," Carver suggested.

Holmes looked around the room and felt humbled. Nearly all hands were up for the strike. All the females, Holly, Katie, Kirsty and Mary had their hands up. Earnshaw had not but he didn't count. Something stirred inside him, a strange feeling. It was the idea of hitting the bully. It was so bloody apt. He had been bullied for so long by Chalmers and the management force behind him. He had never actually hit back. It would feel so good. He thought of his wife and kids and mortgage and waivered. But then suddenly he was part of it again.

"Shit, you know what. This is mad but, who knows, if we all stick together and work as a team. It might work. Is everybody up for this?"

Holmes saw that the only other person who hadn't put his hand up in favour of the walkout was Pete Cowley, the very same Cowley who had devised the stupid table that management was using to make the cuts..

Holmes frowned at him. "Okay Pete, you know, if they decide to halve the news desk, you will be the one to go."

"It's just I've got a wife and kids," he complained. "It will be hell."

"It will be hell alright," Holmes agreed. "But it will be hell alright the other way if management just runs amok and makes cuts. Pete, when I walk out you had just better follow."

THIRTEEN

Like a lot of other elegant buildings in the city centre, Newcastle City Hall belonged to a different age. Even though it was built in the 20th century it paid homage to the 19th and the Victorian buildings of the city's famous architects, Grainger and Dobson. Its interior was comfortable and intimate and had once rocked to the young Beatles on the eve of their conquest of the music industry. It allowed more than 2000 people to share an evening of entertainment.

Tonight the main act was Geoff and Sharpe sat in middle row seats with Mary watching his old pal weave his spell of crude jokes and toilet humour on his audience. He realised Geoff had spotted him from the stage when he started cracking jokes about journalists and how many of them it took to change a light bulb..

Sharpe still couldn't find Geoff's jokes very funny. They were mostly sleazy but seemed to go down well with the large number of tattooed men and women in the hall. His failure to appreciate his friend's stage humour had always been a source of friction between them. He sometimes wondered how they stayed friends.

"Not my cup of tea," Mary told him as lights came on for the interval. "I'm heading for The Rat."

As she spoke Geoff appeared in the aisle signing autographs and winked at Sharpe then put his thumbs up. He handed something to one of the fans and pointed in his direction. The fan dutifully made his way along the row in front and handed him a small envelope. Sharpe opened it to find a backstage pass for after the show for him and a friend.

He put one thumb up to indicate he would be there. Mary was still sitting beside him gazing at the pass. "Does that mean free food and drink if I put up with the remaining hour of this drivel?" she asked brightly.

"I'm guessing it does. But don't be confrontational with my friend will you Mary?"

"Promise." She beamed back at him and he was bedazzled not for the first time by the warmth of her smile. It was growing on him in a way he had not expected. Her hand found his and it felt nice. He couldn't argue with it and they sat that way for the rest of the performance.

They were rewarded afterwards when they were ushered in to a large backstage dressing room along with several other invited fans. A band which had been the second act to Geoff was playing blues music lazily in a corner of the room.

Geoff was still in his stage gear of white paisley shirt and jeans and dabbing the perspiration on his forehead with a towel. "God, it's a hot little place this," he told Sharpe, "like your mum's kitchen used to be on a Sunday."

"Ah yeah, Sunday dinner and Yorkshire puddings, those were the days," Sharpe agreed.

"And the wine for under-age drinkers. That was good too," said Geoff.

He waved a large hand towards a table laden with savouries and bottles. "This is the way I eat these days. Very unhealthy but bloody enjoyable I tell you."

He accepted a large glass of red wine from Geoff while Mary declined and went further down the table for a beer.

"Your girlfriend?" Geoff demanded.

"Work friend. She's Irish by the way so none of those jokes of yours Geoff."

"Ah, I don't do them anymore. I need all the fans I can get. I'm not doing bad you know."

"So I gather."

"What about yourself?"

"So so. You were right about journalism. It's no place for would-be writers."

"No, it's sad. I don't know there is a place for would-be writers these days. They've been replaced by stand-up comics, oh, and chefs of course. The 21st century could certainly do with a literary giant to expose the poverty of some lives but what does it get? Russell Brand! Unbelievable really that a comedian should be the voice of society's underclass, a lost generation of people."

"You're as eloquent as ever Geoff. Does this satisfy you, what you are doing?"'

"It lost its novelty a while back. The fans are always in your face. You want to cut loose but there's always the next show. But hell I'm on my way to making a pile of money. I've got a dvd out soon and there's talk of a possible television show."

"A tv show? That's brilliant."

"Yeah, the tv doesn't know what to do next to stop its audiences deserting it. It's chefs, football, property shows and stand-up comics galore. Nothing very original, I have to admit but that's the way it is. What about you?"

"Well I'm busy working with my friend over there," he gestured to Mary who was now talking to the band members as they grabbed sandwiches, "on an interesting one. This businessman who killed himself. I've met some interesting people, one of them a media student who's financing her studies by working as a hooker or, should I say, high class escort girl."

"She give you a freebie?"

"Geoff, remember that I have sisters."

"Yes, very nice too. I was always envious of you having an older and a younger sister. And both of them adorable."

"Both married now."

"Ah, that's good. Hope they are happy. So this lady of the night, she sounds like a story in herself."

"Yes, she would be if she would go public but she won't. She tells me there's a mansion house in Newcastle where the great and the good avail themselves of the services of girls like her on a regular basis. Lawyers and all kinds of professionals, would you believe?"

Geoff slapped him on the shoulder. "I've been there buddy. I know exactly where it is. I did a private show there a couple of years ago and it wasn't hard to tell there was a lot of swinging going on. The audience kept decreasing as people went upstairs."

Geoff disappeared to the table and came back with more drinks. "Why don't you write about that? Write a book called The Mansion House or The

Big House. People love simple sounding names these days. Say it's based on somewhere you know. Publishers like books written from personal experience. I've got one coming out for Christmas. At home with Geoff Price."

"You're going to be everywhere."

"Yeah, like dog crap I know. Seriously old mate, we are looking at a potential stepping stone for you. I could maybe get you an in with a publisher."

Sharpe fished out a business card. "Well you know I'm interested Geoff. But you're a busy man and it's one thing talking over a drink and it's another thing doing."

"No, I'm serious. I want to help you and I'm bloody bored. I'm surrounded by hangers-on I can't have a decent conversation with. Tell you what I'm going to do. I'm going to put some feelers out and see if I can get booked at this naughty house again. I'll take you along as my assistant. You can circulate, talk to people, get material for your book. Once you have got something published, you have got contacts. You can bounce other ideas off them. It all makes sense."

Sharpe looked at across at Mary, who was still in animated conversation with the band, and wondered what she would think.

"I'm up for it Geoff. Totally.'

He got back to his flat in the early hours but was still too wired to go to bed. He decided to look up Geoff's blog on his laptop.

There it was again. How dare he describe himself as "comedian and writer Geoff Price". What the hell did he write? One line gags? Had he described himself thus just to annoy him, to stick a knife in to his would-be writer ribs.

If so, he had succeeded.

FOURTEEN

The mansion house sat in a large street which shared a small number of huge houses, all of rambling individual design. It was in a neighbourhood which was a haven for the wealthy yet lay just a mile from Newcastle city centre. Its drive was a hundred yards long and dwarfed on each side by towering aspens. It had once been the house of a shipbuilding entrepreneur in the heyday of the Tyne river.

Sharpe entered as a passenger in a chauffeur-driven hire limousine. Geoff sat in the front and Sharpe shared the backseat with Nick, his stage manager. He was Nick's assistant for the evening and Nick was not very happy about it. Problem was that neither man could tell him the real reason he was there. Geoff had told him that Sharpe wanted a taste of the life of a stand-up comic as he was thinking of becoming one. Nick had shown his disbelief in this story with a withering glance in Sharpe's direction.

He had been given a small badge to wear which said assistant. It was a Sunday and the clocks had just gone forward to summertime. A smiling and smartly dressed bouncer welcomed them by opening their car doors as they arrived at the front entrance porch which was part of a large Victorian conservatory. The house was a rambling Gothic folly full of turrets and arches and windows of al shapes and sizes. They seemed to walk for ages through endless passages until they were in the concert room which was big and high-ceilinged with a raised stage. A grand piano sat in the corner of a stage and Nick immediately hopped on to it to check out the sound system for the evening. A large open fire and tiled mantelpiece formed the centre of the room which was full of oak tables all of them occupied by guests.

"I usually have a pint just to relax my nerves a little beforehand," said Geoff, guiding him to the bar. "It gives me a little lift."

They joined a queue around the bar and Geoff got two pints of bitter. The pair stood supping, Geoff talking endlessly as he geared himself up for his show, Sharpe slowly surveying the guests in the room. It was not an ordinary assembly of everyday folk. There were no children. There were just one or two elderly men who had an air of importance about them. Sharpe wondered if one of them might be the judge. The rest of the guests were young and middle-aged men and women. Some were couples but a lot were not. There was an air of sexual excitement and Sharpe wondered if a stripper might not have been the most appropriate entertainment, not a standup.

A woman was staring at him so intensely from across the room that he felt uncomfortable. Then he realised it was Felicity. Her face was a question. "What the hell are you doing here?" it said. He was relieved when the lights dimmed and the master of ceremonies took the stage. The mc boomed a welcome to the audience and promised them they were in for a treat. Geoff handed him his empty glass and headed for the backstage. The mc warmed people up with a couple of little gags of his own and then Geoff was up and working, trotting out his jokes which, to Sharpe, were like the ones you got inside Christmas crackers only with a lot of smut attached.

He decided to explore and wandered out of the main chamber in to another room also served by a bar. There was a newspaper stand, some comfortable sofas and two full size snooker tables. There were only a few people at the bar so Sharpe wandered up and ordered himself another pint of bitter.

"This your first time here?" The question was from a fellow lone drinker at the bar. Sharpe turned to find a smiling man giving him a friendly grin. He was immaculately dressed in a dark blue silk suit and tie and had a suntan that suggested he spent a lot of time away from the north of England.

"I'm here with the comedian, helping him out. Got nothing to do while he is on stage," the explanation had been carefully rehearsed with Geoff just in case there were problems.

"Yes, you look like a fish out of water, if you don't mind me saying. Do you feel uncomfortable in this place?"

"Just a little. I've heard some funny stories about it."

"Yes, it's got a bit of a reputation around the city, a place where swingers congregate and sex is rampant. Actually it's not like that. I've been coming here for years but not for sex. It's a club. It tried to be an exclusive gentlemen's club like the ones in London but it just didn't stay that way. They should never have let those premiership footballers in. That's when the escort agencies got the sniff of big money."

"So there is some swinging. Is it true it's run by a judge?"

"Not run. The business is owned by a judge who spends all his time in London these days. He just turns a blind eye. The actual place is set up so discreet that it tends to be above the law. That's why even the police use it, some of their most senior officers. God, they've got a red-blooded appetite those boys. Food, drink and ladies all the way."

Sharpe couldn't believe his luck. He had only been in the place ten minutes and he had found someone more than ready and willing to give him the lowdown on it.

"George is my name by the way. Do you want another drink?" He called for two more pints and scanned the room again trying not to look nervous. No sign of Felicity.

"I'm Simon. Simon Thompson. How this place works is on two levels if you like, the what you see level and the what you can't see level. We members are free to wander everywhere apart from the top floor where the green rooms are. That's run like a Japanese karaoke hall. There's a key desk. You hire a room and get a key for it. You can lock yourself away and do what you like while the karaoke is playing. There's a telephone service which brings you anything you want, drink, food, condoms."

"And you've never used it."

"No, honestly," Simon put a hand on his heart. "I'm not being vain. I have never needed to pay for sex. It usually finds me. I come here to meet interesting people and there are a lot of interesting people use this place. I'm a banker so I can make useful contacts and bankers need to do a bit of PR with the public these days after all the calamities that have gone on."

"I'm told that Jim Jones was a regular here," Sharpe played his cards and waited for the response. His new friend seemed to buckle at the knees. He placed both hands on the bar as if bracing himself.

"You alright?"

"My friend, if poor Jim was alive right now he would be here standing with us. He was a regular at this bar. Did you know him?"

"No, I just read about him. I heard he used to get in here."

"Such a shame. I just wish he had come to me about his money troubles. He knew I was a banker. But he never mentioned anything. He liked to have a few drinks at this very bar. I have to say Jim was a green room man. He tended to divide his attention between drink and the girls, so many different girls. But then he had loads of money, or so it seemed. There was a little clique of them. You would think at times they were in a competition to pull different women."

Geoff's voice had stopped and the applause was lukewarm. Simon spotted someone he knew and was waving to catch his attention. Sharpe looked in the same direction to see his editor Chalmers shuffling in to the room. "Here's one of that lot now," Simon confided.

"Nice meeting you Simon but I have to dash to help onstage. See you next time." Sharpe was away without even a handshake, walking in the opposite direction to his editor so that he would not be recognised.

Geoff was back at the bar in the main room, pint in hand and talking to a strikingly well-dressed couple, the man in a dinner jacket and the woman in a full length gown. Nick was on stage tidying up.

He headed straight for the exit door where he ran in to Felicity looking stunning in a turquoise mini dress.

"What the hell are you doing here," she demanded.

"It's a long story."

"You're not spying on me are you? You're not going to snatch a picture of me for your paper or anything like that?"

"No, I promise. Nothing like that. It's not about you."

"You know George I wasn't joking when I offered you a freebie. I think you and I could be good together.

"I just need to get away from here quick Felicity. There's a person I can't afford to be spotted by."

"Come with me. I'll take you to the green rooms."

She put out her hand to him. He was in such a panic he took it and allowed himself to be led to the lift. Once inside it, she was pressing up to him, her hair falling on his shoulders. He guiltily put an arm around here.

Once out of the lift they were in a small brightly lit room adorned with one sofa and coffee table and an unmanned desk. Felicity rang a bell on the desk and an attendant in a green uniform appeared from nowhere.

"I'll have a room please," she ordered and fished some notes out of her bag.

"Room 25 madam," the man smiled at her as he handed her the keys and nodded at George. It was just like booking in to a posh hotel. How the rich could live.

Felicity grabbed his hand and led him along a long corridor to room 25. Once inside she turned down the Michael Jackson song emanating from a huge tv and speakers. There was a bottle of wine in a bucket on a corner table and she poured two large glasses.

"I'm going to have a shower in the bedroom," she announced. Sharpe took refuge in his glass of wine as he tried to think out his next move. Chalmers would be here for some time. He couldn't get out. He tapped out Geoff's number on his mobile and got an immediate response.

"Where the hell are you?" his friend demanded. "We've been looking for you. We're all at the car waiting to go."

"Sorry, it's complicated. I can't come with you. I'm in one of the green rooms."

"What, you've picked up a woman. That was quick work." Geoff's tone had changed from anger to admiration. All was okay in the world. "Give me a bell in the morning. I've got something important to tell you." The phone died.

Felicity wandered back in to the room in a silver silk dressing gown.

FIFTEEN

Sharpe felt a bit jaded next morning and was nodding off behind a copy of the Times when his phone made him jump involuntarily. It was Geoff.

"Mmmmmorning Geoff, I thought I was supposed to ring you."

"Couldn't wait. I've got a hot one for you man. I was talking to a couple at the bar after my act. I think they were the only ones there who liked it."

"Yes, I saw them. Dressed up to the eyeballs."

"That's them. Now don't knock it. That very well dressed gentleman was the top dog in the Northumbria police force, chief constable until he retired a year ago. He knows a thing or two."

"Okay, I'm listening."

"Well he hears everything that's going on and is very press friendly, so he tells me. Now the new chief constable rings him nearly every week for some advice about something or other. You know what they are like, these top dogs, worried sick about making a mistake. Anyway, this means that my new found friend from last night is privy to a lot of confidential stuff about what is going on. So, listen to this. That guy you were talking about, Jim Jones."

Sharpe was suddenly very attentive to what his friend was saying. "Yes, what about him?"

"There was a lot of guff going about concerning his wife and kids, how she had left him and blah de blah. Well, that's all crap. The police are quite worried about the three of them but have kept it low key. Now this Jones guy had a second home, a part of an old castle up in the Scottish borders, about ten miles north of the border I think. Yesterday the maintenance guy is checking the level of the oil tank that they use to supply the heating. There's quite a few of the nouveau riche living in this castle and the heating is all oil-fired so it is a huge tank. The indicator on the side of the tank is not showing him anything so he has to take the roof of the tank off and look inside. He sees a body propped up against the side of the wall to the level indicator. The police come and empty the tank and find three bodies in all, two of them small. It's the talk of the force George. This guy was so hot with it last night. Only thing is that it's in the hands of the Scottish lot and they are not naming names until the Scottish version of the coroner, the whatshisname?

"The procurator fiscal."

"That's him. They are not naming names until he has got his report. But it's wide open for you man. Just go for it, I would say. No more redundancy worries."

"Thanks Geoff. I don't know how I will pay you back."

"Hey, we're not done yet. There's your book right. I'm going to have a word with my publisher."

"Sounds good."

"Yeah, my publisher HarperCollins. Standups are the new face of society, telling it like it is. My life story, would you believe."

"So that's how you call yourself a writer. I knew you when you had very little."

"Yes, writing jokes on the backs of bus tickets. They're not laughing at me now, as Bob Monkhouse used to say. Look George. I'm not going to get bigheaded about it. I'm going to milk it for what it's worth then get out. You don't fancy South America by car do you?"

"No, motor bike, Che Guevara style."

"Hah, hah. Listen. Don't be afraid to go to the top for your story today. My friend from last night says the new Northumbria chief is also very press friendly. He says just be bold. Stuff the press office and everybody else. Ring Bill Fawcett, the head of the force, tell him what you have heard and how you'd like to help the investigation or something like that. I even think this guy is going to mention you to him beforehand because I asked for that. Good luck and I'll look forward to reading tonight's paper."

Sharpe put down the phone and composed himself. He knew he had to play this cool and act quickly but he didn't want to be out manoeuvred by the other vultures in the newsroom. He would bypass Cowley and go straight to Holmes. But first he would ring Bill Fawcett at force HQ in Ponteland.

He was put through almost immediately by a super efficient switchboard operator. A gruff voice demanded: "Fawcett. Who's this?"

He introduced himself, trying to sound relaxed. It seemed to work when the voice of the chief also became more casual.

"I understand there's been a development in the Jim Jones case in relation to his family."

"So what have you heard young man?"

He outlined everything that Geoff had told him and was allowed to talk uninterrupted for a couple of minutes.

"Okay young man. I hear everything you say and I have also heard a little about you. You are fairly new in your job but you're an honest fellow, I'm told. So here's the deal. I can't possibly give you an official comment on this. My own position will be in jeopardy if I do. But I will help you and I would ask you to protect my position on this. You're on the right track and if you run a story on the lines that the bodies are believed to be those of blah, blah, blah, the wife and kids of this man you will be right. It's just the bloody Scottish side is so lethargic on this. So, if you trust me, you can stick your neck out without worrying too much about your head being chopped off. But no references to a senior police source even today. Tomorrow might be different and I would expect you to call me."

The chief put the phone down without a goodbye. Sharpe checked all his notes and made sure he had them in good order. He looked up to see that Cowley was at the coffee machine and Holmes was yawning at the command desk. It was an ideal moment and he zipped over.

Homes looked tired and grimaced at him when he arrived. "I hope this is not a problem, George. I'm up to my eyeballs in it at the minute. This firm has gone mad."

Sharpe refused to be sidetracked and spelt out his story of the day. As he spoke the tiredness seemed to lift from Holmes and his eyes acquired a sparkle. When he had finished Holmes was just sitting beaming.

"George I don't know what you are running on these days but I could do with some in my tank, I tell you. It must be all these women, is it?"

Sharpe flushed slightly wondering how much gossip had got out about his trip to the green rooms. How could anyone possibly know about it?

Holmes spared him any further blushes and told him to bash out his story pronto. "Let it run, George. Let it bloody run."

SIXTEEN

Holmes had failed to turn in for work. It was unheard of. His hundred per cent attendance record had never been compromised by a sick note. There was a general malaise about the newsroom. Cowley sat in his chair, czar for the day, but no one could take him seriously. Chalmers prowled around the command desk but for once said very little.

Sharpe was despondent. He had been moving steadily up the league of death, leap frogging another reporter every day much to Cowley's unconcealed annoyance. He had dominated four front pages in a row with his stories about the Jones deaths thanks to his new informant, the chief constable. He was about to claim top spot for the fifth day running with his latest follow-up but it simply wasn't the same without Holmes nurturing him on and beaming when they got the result. On completion of the story he walked over to the desk and bypassed Cowley speaking directly to Chalmers, a man he had lost all respect for after spotting him in the mansion house. Talking to him bluntly was therefore so much easier.

"Seems to me, that someone needs to find out what's wrong with Phil," he said. "I don't mind doing it. I'm concerned." He was aware of a look of undisguised hostility from Cowley who wagged his head in the negative. "Just get back to your job Sharpe. Do what you're told."

"I've done the Jones story for today Cowley, if you care to check onscreen, so, if you don't mind, I would like to get on with something else."

Chalmers gave him a little grin. "Ah, you're the man these days Mr Sharpe. All these great stories. From a very slow start, you've gone off like a rocket. I wish I could say the same for more of the staff."

Chalmers turned and gazed at Cowley as he spoke. Cowley blanched and gazed down at his lists.

"Yes, go on. I like people to show initiative and if you think it's the right thing to do, get out there and found out what the hell is going on with him. I've not had a call or anything."

Duly despatched, Sharpe wasted no time in leaving the newsroom. His only problem was that he was without his own car which had failed to start for him that morning.

That meant a time wasting trip to the Metro Edifice garage where there was a fleet of Astra saloons which were the pool cars used by the photographers and reporters.

Each battered car had its own history of minor bumps and scrapes to tell. To get one out on to the street, the driver had to negotiate a series of narrow ramps and, under deadline pressure, care was often abandoned and cars scraped.

The photographers were the worst. A photographer could spend hours in a car on the hunt for the right picture. Newspapers, half-eaten sandwiches and banana skins would be discarded on the floor and, just for good measure, cigarette ash dumped in the glove compartments of the car doors.

Sharpe guessed that the car he had been given had last been used by Dave Jennings a heavy smoker. Not only was it a disgusting mess but the stench of smoke made him feel like puking. He wound down both front windows and breathed deeply as he headed for the city's Chapel Dene estate for a word with Holmes' wife. He felt fairly relaxed about it as he had met Sue Holmes once before in The Rat. He had been struck by how friendly she was, considering she had to share her life with a permanently grimfaced news editor, and surmised that Holmes must have a better side to his nature.

The estate was a 1980s style sprawl of fairly large semi-detached house with gated drives which made it easy to park. Within a minute he was knocking at the door of number 19. It was answered by a jam-faced boy and Sharpe checked his watch. It was 8.30am, the school run. The boy ran off to get his mum and Sue appeared at the door smiling.

"Oh, has that daft husband of mine left something behind," she asked and Sharpe felt shivers in the base of his spine.

"Er no, Sue. Nothing like that . . . ." He searched for the right words but they wouldn't come. Her face turned white in realisation that something was wrong. "Please, what is it?" she insisted.

"He's not there, not at work," he blurted out the words. He felt useless.

"My God. What can it be?" She put her hand to her mouth. Her son was suddenly at her side and she put her arms around him. "This is just ridiculous. I just can't think. He just went off on his bike as usual."

Sharpe was amazed to hear that his boss cycled to work but disguised his surprise. "I'm really sorry to have bothered you like this. I think I had better just go back to the office and see if we know anymore."

She nodded. Tears were flowing and she couldn't find words. She closed the door and Sharpe walked quickly to his car wanting to be out of the street as quickly as possible. He parked a couple of blocks away and rang in. It was Cowley who answered. He listened to what he had to say without showing any sign of concern about his partner on the news desk.

"Just get back to the office now," was all he said.

It was no good, he thought as he drove back to the city. Cowley was in charge yet he was inadequate for the task. And he, George Sharpe, could not work with him anyway. Something had to give.

When he got back to his desk, he rang Fawcett. The chief listened patiently to what he had to say and promised to run a check on the incidents of the day to see if anything turned up but it was, he said, a fairly quiet day.

Sharpe had an idea and went back over to the desk. "Shall we run a piece in the paper about this? It's kind of a mystery disappearance at the moment and I think Phil would probably expect it of us really."

Chalmers and Cowley both looked at him as if he was mad.

"He's one of us," said Chalmers coldly. "We are not going to do anything to upset his family right now. We leave them alone and that's it."

Sharpe couldn't believe what he was hearing. The news editor of The Metropolis was missing and its editor had just ordered a blackout on news of his disappearance.

"Isn't that a bit two-faced?" he said angrily. "One rule for Joe Public, who's fair game, and another for us."

"That's enough," Chalmers ordered. "You're in a good position now Mr Sharpe. A position of job security compared to some others. Don't blow it. There's always plenty of people in the dole queues you know."

SEVENTEEN

Sharpe was dangling Cowley out of the third floor window of The Metropolis, more by accident than design. He hated violence and fighting but it had all got out of hand. Cowley's eyes were terrified slits and he was pleading for his life. He had called Sharpe in to Chalmers's office for a private word and things had gone crazy. Chalmers was on a day off and Cowley had taken the opportunity to use his office for one-to-ones with all the reporters. Things were going to be different now that he was in charge. That was the message.

Sharpe had felt uneasy in the newsroom ever since Holmes had disappeared from it. The lily-faced, studious, beer loving Holmes was not the friendliest of souls but Sharpe had begun to realise just how good he was as a mentor to him now that he was absent. He was not warming to Cowley at all and felt that the ever smiling acting news editor was speaking unkindly about him behind his back.

This was confirmed when Cowley told him that he was still in the danger zone despite all the good stories he had recently produced. "I think you have just been lucky at the right time. You had been absolutely hopeless up until the last week or so."

The harsh words were too much for Sharpe who had started asking a few questions of Cowley about his capabilities. He started haranguing him about his League of Death and how irresponsible it was. Cowley countered by calling him a dreamer who would never write anything useful. The next thing the two men were grappling silently over the desk of the office, each trying to gauge each other's strength, the outside world oblivious to what was going on. "I'm a karate black belt you know Sharpe," Cowley had warned him. Sharpe had countered with an old judo throw he remembered which bounced Cowley off the fax machine and out of the window behind it. Sharpe had been trained to always hold on to the lapels of the person you threw so as not to do him too much damage and this saved Cowley from plunging around 20 metres to the pavement below where pedestrians wandered along on their various missions of the day unaware of the drama above.

Cowley was clutching his arms with a quivering grip. Sharpe felt dizzy as he hung on to the lapels of Cowley's blue suit for dear life. He could see lamp standards and a wheely bin below and resolved that if the new news editor of The Metropolis was to slip from his grasp he would try and guide him to miss them. Cowley began to whimper: "Don't drop me please George," he said, using his Christian name for the first time. "Please please don't drop me."

Cowley had bright blue eyes sunk in an English heartland face and his cheeks of roast beef pink were now dark crimson. He was a blubbering, wild-eyed coward and Sharpe began enjoying his moment. If only he could video record it and put it on facebook.

"Hah, no longer the king eh?" Sharpe mocked him. "Now you're on the receiving end. Now you can feel the fear that you inflict on others, you bastard. I've had enough of your sort of po-faced domineering gutless little administrators. You think you can rule the roost by making everyone scared for their jobs well I'm not having it. You can have some back."

"For Christ's sake George, think about getting me back in to the office. You'll be on a murder charge otherwise."

"You're in a bit of a mess yourself at the minute. Never mind about me."

Sharpe was jubilant at finally bringing Cowley to his knees. There had never been any love lost between them. He had never used the old judo move he was taught at university in real combat. But all the months of practice from years ago had been worth it. It was like riding a bike. You never forgot something like that.

"I have a very strong temper which does not often manifest itself," he told Cowley. "But it is lethal when it does."

"Yes, yes, I see that," said Cowley meekly: "Please just get me inside."

Sharpe hauled Cowley back through the window and stood his quivering form against the fax like a large ornament. Then he planted one neat punch on his jaw with all the strength he could manage. Cowley staggered around the fax machine and went down like the Titanic taking trays of paper clips and drawing pins with him with a wave of his outstretched arm. He hit the floor and lay quite still. Sharpe wondered if he was dead or alive. He didn't much care either way.

He walked out of the editor's office in to the newsroom. Mary Rainwell was watching him from behind her desktop. "You look a bit dishevelled, to say the least. What's going on?" she demanded.

"Come for a coffee and I'll explain." He couldn't help sounding a bit cocky.

Rea, Vince, 28, died suddenly ....

SIX a.m. The phone snapped him awake in the darkness of his bedroom. The ice cold voice of Cowley killed his dream. "Can you get in here quick Sharpe? There's a job for you."

The sunrises were getting earlier and by the time he parked the car it was a pleasant walk in to the office where Cowley was waiting for him with a one line death notice from that morning's newspaper that said Vince Reay, 28, died suddenly. An address was handwritten on the paper.

Sharpe was immediately suspicious. There were already a half dozen other reporters in the office so why was Cowley so desperate to send Sharpe, a reporter he disliked, on this job. He couldn't ask the question as it would give Cowley more ammunition to make him look foolish. He set off on his job but as he walked through the newsroom Tony Carver caught his eye and called him over.

"Are you going out on this Vince Reay death?" he demanded.

Sharpe nodded and showed him the death notice. Carver wagged his head and sighed.

"You know, I hate this type of devious stuff. Something needs to be done."

"Tad rebellious today Tony."

Carver glared at him with a deadly serious face.

"Look that bloke over there is dangerous," he said quietly, nodding towards Cowley. "I have already told him all about this one and he tells you nothing."

Cowley was now staring at the two men. Carver smiled and winked at him. "Just talking football," he shouted across.

"This man Reay is one of the biggest villains in Newcastle," he told Sharpe quietly. "He ran one of the biggest two crime gangs and has without doubt been executed by the other gang. He was shot in the head as he sat in a West End pub enjoying his last pint."

"Christ. Oh well at least I won't feel uncomfortable about the knock. I won't be intruding on the lives of a nice respectable family."

Carver grimaced. "Reay's cronies are deadly. You need to watch your step. I have offered to approach the family with the help of some backup from my friendly cops but that bugger over there won't have any. For some reason he wants you out on this job."

"Yeah, I know the reason. He doesn't like me and wants to make me look stupid."

Carver smiled. "Yes, at least you have no illusions about your standing with him."

"No, I know he hates my guts. I had a dream about him last night where I nearly killed him."

"It's probably what he needs. There have been fights in this place before George. I remember one news editor who threatened an editor with a chair leg."

"I've no doubt. Kind of a lawless world, the fourth estate. I find it hard to like it."

"It has a purpose George. It does some good work. Who else would keep the headcases that run our society in order?"

"I guess that's true but today I am on the dark side of it. Wish me luck."

Carver smiled: "It might be a good day to say you got no answer on the doorstep."

"I'll think about it."

The pleasant nature of the day was now lost on Sharpe as he drove to Sycamore Street in the city's west end. He was now contemplating his immediate welfare if the job got nasty. There were unstable people around who could dish out violence at the drop of a hat and he had a feeling he was going to meet some today. But he was going to do the knock.

There was no chickening out. He was now driving through an estate of straight rows of terraced houses, some well kept some rundown, social housing. Every now and then one of them was completely boarded up. These properties would mostly belong to private landlords willing to buy property cheap and get their rent on a direct debit from the welfare services.

He found the address, a ground floor flat, and surveyed its exterior. It was a modest place but tidy, no rubbish in the small front garden and a window cleaner had called recently. This fitted in with what Carver had told him about Vince Reay. He had left his wife and their large gated home in the suburbs to start a relationship with the woman who lived here, a nurse. When the gang of thugs who were his enemies realised how easy it was to get him they did.

Sharpe looked for a bell to ring but could not find one. He tried not to make too much noise with the large metal knocker on the front door, just enough to be heard. After some time and some noises of conversation inside the flat, the door was slowly opened. A white-faced woman in a dressing gown stared blankly at him.

"Hello, I am really sorry to bother you at a time like this but I am from The Metropolis newspaper and wondered if the family would care to talk about what has happened."

The woman blinked at him, glanced behind her in to the interior and spoke quickly. "I'm Louise's sister. She's really too upset to talk to the press but, if I was you, I would leg it because you're about the seventh reporter here today and Vince's lads beat the last one up."

As she spoke, Sharpe heard yelling and screaming inside the flat. The woman turned but was brushed aside by a huge shaven-headed man in T-shirt and jeans. There was another man behind him who looked equally fearsome. Shaven-head caught Sharpe's shoulder, spinning him round. He swung a blow which hit Sharpe's shoulder instead of his intended target, the face. The force of the blow staggered him and he knew flight was the only answer if he wanted to avoid being bounced off the pavement by thugs. He ran straight past the company car he had parked in the street. He knew if he stopped to try and open the door they would have him.

Sharpe headed in the direction of Newcastle city centre and ran over a flyover walkway pursued by the thugs. Walkers stopped to stare at this relatively smartly dressed man being pursued by two shaven head ex-convicts who were swearing their heads off.

Sharpe was trying to pace himself. It was a race he had to win. Market Street police station was probably the best place to head for. He glanced behind to see his pursuers were still at the same distance and showing no signs of giving up the chase. He was about to cross the street when his path was blocked by a white Astra. Its door was flung open and a booming voice shouted: "Get in you idiot."

Sharpe recognised it as the voice of Tony Carver and hopped in to the passenger seat. Carver put his foot down and turned towards him. "I told you it would be trouble, didn't I."

EIGHTEEN

G areth Chalmers sat in the oak panelled executive dining room of the Metropolis, picking at his lunch, a tuna bake. He was reading a copy of his newspaper. It looked brilliant, a top story with pictures about a triple murderer businessman, some great follow-ups to other deaths like the squaddie killed in Afghanistan. Pictures, sidebars and factfiles galore. The pot was full and boiling hot. The Metropolis was wiping out the competition it faced in the city. But Chalmers felt down. He was worried.

Although he would never bother to tell anyone as much, Gareth Chalmers had not been a good newspaper reporter. He had found the newsroom too noisy and too challenging as a young trainee reporter and had very quickly decided to join the studious types on the sub-editors' table who sat quietly all day at their work, cutting and revising the stories brought in by reporters. The sub-editors' table formed the time honoured pathway to an editorship. Chalmers liked the feeling of control over the newspaper's contents. He didn't understand the reporters who formed the frontline of the news gathering service. He had always seen them as utterly expendable. He regarded himself as a colonel in total command of the battlefield who had to think ahead and use his troops and ammunition wisely. He had always relied on a good sergeant to run the frontline. That sergeant was Phil Holmes and Holmes had disappeared leaving a bunch of reporters talking about staging a walkout. They had always done what they were told. Why were they complicating things? Didn't they understand that when higher management ordered cuts it was for a reason?

Chalmers had grown so bad-humoured about the newspaper that his wife started to ignore him on his return from work. He would sit in the kitchen after dinner polishing off a bottle of claret while she disappeared in to the conservatory to read until late. Weekends were no longer the same. His wife would now not cook when he had his friends around to ply them with the beer and wine left-overs he smuggled home after boardroom functions. In return they listened to his tales of daring and audacity in shaping the vibrant column inches of his newspaper, the unprintable inside stories that the staff knew but couldn't publish because it was a family newspaper. Like the story of a well known elderly magistrate who had been found dead in his bathroom. The paper's story said mystery surrounded the death. But there was no mystery. It was just an unprintable fact that the man had suffered a heart attack while pleasuring himself in the privacy of his own bathroom. He had held court a few times with that story.

Chalmers had started going out to get away from his wife. He even drove the car after polishing off the claret. His wife harangued him every time but he ignored her. He was untouchable, invincible.

No-one could bring him down. He started going to the city's expensive bars where he would end up rubbing shoulders with wealthy Premiership footballers. He had returned once more to the mansion house and the wonderful women who worked there. It was a place he knew well but had decided to stop visiting because of the risk to his reputation. But he had gone back and started to run up a bill that he would have to sort out quickly before it became a problem for him. Chalmers wondered where it was all heading.

Something was gnawing away at him. He couldn't put his finger on it but deep down he had a feeling he should be worried. Phil Holmes and his team had been coming up with some belter stories lately. They had made the competition look rubbish. That young fellow Sharpe had been a revelation. His stories were incredible. How would he replace these good hard news reporters if they walked out?

Of course, there were always trainees hammering on the door to take their place but, as he had heard Tony Carver saying many times, in the bar after work, anyone can be a reporter but a good newspaper needs operators, people who can come up with the goods time after time in all kinds of situations.

If he sacked the bad half of his reporters he would be left without the good half as well. That's what Holmes and company had told him and Holmes had been so unpleasant about it. He was asking to be sacked but who could replace him, not that idiot Cowley.

It had taken a potential strike to make him realise how valuable his reporters were. He had started to see them as the goal-scoring strikers in his team and his sub-editors the defenders. At the moment the goals were flying in but they wouldn't continue to unless they both turned up and played well.

Chalmers reluctantly tried another forkful of tuna but was interrupted by the purple face of Owen Michaelson which brought him to prompt attention. Michaelson was the London-based managing director of the Metropolis consortium. Chalmers had never seen him before in the flesh but knew his face from the monthly video conferences between the Newcastle and London operations. What the hell was he doing in Newcastle? This meant nothing but trouble. Chalmers had never been troubled by the company's top national executives before. His own regional managing director, Olwen Hardy, was responsible for both the Newcastle and Dublin operations of the company. As she was Irish, she spent all her time in Dublin and not on his doorstep. That had been great for him but now he had Michaelson on his case without a word of warning from her.

Michaelson was a blunt Yorkshireman who bragged that a good advertising sales person was worth three journalists when it came to newspaper profitability. Profitability was his only yardstick.

"What the hell is going on?" Michaelson demanded as Chalmers folded his newspaper and gave up on his lunch. " The Venezuelans are itchy. Robert Morton is on the warpath.

"Pardon?" Chalmers couldn't help sounding a little indignant but the m.d. continued his tirade.

"What the fuck is going on in Newcastle with your newspaper Chalmers?" To emphasize his point Michaelson picked up the folded newspaper that Chalmers had just put down and slapped it on the table. "There's all kinds of bloody talk reaching me about silly stuff. Who's this Mrs Williamson and what the hell was that reporter Earnshaw doing in her house with a bible? We are not stupid down in London you know. We have lines of communication you wouldn't dream of. And I'm not talking about Olwen bloody Hardy."

Chalmers stiffened his face in to its most serious yet dignified setting and tried to offset the tirade. "Ah, we are dealing with that. I've spoken to Earnshaw. He went too far."

"You've spoken to him? You should have had him shot! Mrs Williamson has sent a full account to the board. She says she is taking her case to the industry regulator because you have done nothing about it. This journalist goes in to her house and steals from her and you spoke to him."

"Earnshaw is no longer with us. He was a bad egg. I got rid of him," Chalmers lied.

"Mrs Williamson doesn't know that. I have spoken to her myself. She has had no meaningful communication from you Chalmers. If you had contacted her as editor and, bearing in mind the gravity of what she claims there was every reason for you to do so, she would not be going to the regulator. All you did was send around some young girl reporter to try and calm her down and she saw right through that."

"She hasn't contacted me."

"She contacted whatshisname, the chap who disappeared. He's your news editor. He would have told you of the seriousness of what Earnshaw did to her. Don't try to deny that's the case Chalmers."

"I can't actually sir," Chalmers admitted, slumping in his seat.

"Look, this is bad, a clear intrusion on somebody and a crime to boot, " Michaelson was unstoppable. " You haven't been taking this seriously enough and also word reaches me from our competitors that you are operating some kind of league of death up there. Is that true?"

Chalmers was shell-shocked but resolved that he was not going down for that stupid league table that Eddie Black had told him about.

"Sorry sir, but I have no idea on that one. I can look in to it by all means. You know, I can't know what every reporter is doing from one minute to the next."

"Do you send your reporters out to doorstep people cold, like salesmen, as soon as a death notice appears in the paper Chalmers?"

"Well no, we usually need more information from the police or the coroner's officer, an idea of what it is. It's a very sensitive area."

"Yeah sounds like a very sensitive area that you drive a tank full of reporters in to every day Chalmers. Look I'm not daft. I've been down to classified sales this morning and spoken to its head of department Alan Jones. He said they keep getting the odd telephone call from journalists desperate to find an address for a death in the paper. If this is going on, it's another indictment of your editorial style of management Chalmers. I think you should be a very worried man."

"Yes sir."

"I've been brushing up on the journalists' code of conduct Chalmers. Doesn't it say something about not intruding in to private grief."

Chalmers repeated the exact words:" A journalist does nothing to intrude into anybody's private life, grief or distress unless justified by overriding consideration of the public interest"

"Yes, exactly. But I don't think that's being observed in Newcastle Chalmers. And I'm going to change things around so that it is. Consider your job very much under the microscope here."

"Yes sir," Chalmers nodded glumly. He needed to tell Michaelson about the impending reporters' strike but now was not the time.

"Get me Black and Cowley and get them bloody quick," Chalmers rasped to Liz Saunders as he strutted back in to his office. He had taken a mauling from Michaelson and was a wounded man. It was time to bang some heads together.

Cowley was the first to arrive, flashing the usual dazzling smile he reserved for his boss.

"What the fuck is going on with your newsdesk Cowley?" Chalmers demanded.

The smile was replaced by a rising tide of crimson around Cowley's cheeks.

"What boss? I don't know what you mean."

" London has been on to me. They say that the word is that some kind of league of death is being operated up here. Is that true?"

Cowley was now scarlet."Well yes boss. It's the league table that I compile every day. I thought you knew about it."

Edddie Black strolled in to the office to save Cowley's blushes. "Oh no, the boss doesn't know about it Pete. I just took it on as a performance management task."

Chalmers feigned huge surprise. "You knew about this Eddie? You knew about this league that I have just been stitched up with by London?"

"Well yes boss," Black had remembered his brief well. "I didn't think you would be interested. I thought you would just want me to look after it."

Chalmers raised his voice to a level that would carry to all in the newsroom outside. "If this has been going on, it's a serious indictment of your editorial style of management Black. I think you should be a very worried man."

Black was transfixed in the hostile stare from Chalmers who now dropped his voice to a whisper. "Now you two, if this has been going on I want all evidence of it destroyed at once because this is not going to sink my ship. There's to be no mention of it by anybody. If it comes to it Eddie, you will have to face the music."

Black suddenly sprang to life. He had been thinking long and hard about Phil Holmes' call for action over cuts and felt it was time to make a stand. He had been an outsider in Newcastle for too long. He had nothing to lose. If he sided with the reporters he might even make some friends and he also fancied Kirsty. Chalmers was astonished to note an edge of hostility in his voice.

"Does that mean the redundancies amongst the reporters no longer apply?"

"The proposed redundancies were always based on under-performance Eddie. What on earth do you mean?"

"Sorry to have to tell you this boss but they were based on the league of death," Black was staring angrily at his editor. "And another thing you should know by now. The buck always stops at the top, doesn't it boss? Not even you can avoid that happening even if you didn't know about what was going on."

NINETEEN

Sharpe nursed his left shoulder, rubbing it until the pain eased. Carver, for once, was not talkative. He had never known the big man so quiet. Maybe he had something on his mind. After they had parked the car, he found out what it was.

"I'm calling a meeting today George. These cuts are still on the cards and I don't think this management should be allowed to get away with it. They think that now that Holmes is out of the picture we won't do anything. We have to call their bluff. Do I have your support."

"Hell, yes," said Sharpe. "I've just been in a near death situation for the sake of those bastards and they are playing about with us. I think Mary will be okay as well."

Carver grinned. "Oh, you can speak for Mary now, just like her better half, eh."

"She's a friend."

"I think there's more than that."

"Just a friend, honest."

They had entered the newsroom and Mary was approaching, on her way out of the office. When she saw Sharpe she shouted at him.

"You swine. You stayed the night with that tart didn't you."

Sharpe felt a punch to the arm he had been nursing and winced in a new bout of pain.

"Stop it Mary, that hurts. What are you on about?"

"You slept with that Felicity. Your mate has been looking for you. He can't stop talking about it."

"Geoff?"

"Yes, Geoff. He can't stop talking about the exploits of his Casanova pal, the swordsman of the Metropolis. He's going to mention you in his act. And he asks me if I want to do a story about you?"

Mary's face was red with anger. Tony Carver was trying hard not to laugh. "And you say you're just friends. I don't believe it," he said.

"It's not like that Mary. We didn't sleep together. I've got sisters. I don't do things like that."

"Well what did you do?"

"We talked, honest. Maybe I can see you after work, have a drink. I'll tell you all about it. Right now I have something to do."

Mary marched on her way. Sharpe made for the command desk where Cowley was sitting and waiting for him with his usual look of contemptuous impatience.

"Well, how did it go?"

"It went exactly like this," Sharpe explained as he swung his good fist in to Cowley's face. Blood spurted from his nose and he squealed at the pain.

"That's for sending me on a job where I was attacked. You knew there was a risk of it so you can have your share."

Pandemonium broke out in the newsroom. Chalmers appeared followed by two of his sub-editors. The two subs got hold of one arm each of Sharpe as if they planned to throw him out of the building.

"I'm not going to hit him again," Sharpe explained. "I only got punched once and I just wanted to share it with him."

Tony Carver had also appeared by his side. Cowley, still in his seat, was moaning for his life's worth like a felled footballer trying to get his opponent the red card. Telephones were going unanswered.

"It's just handbags," said Carver, flashing a big smile, "A little training ground spat."

"I can't have fighting in the office," said Chalmers. "We've got a school group arriving in a minute for a show around the building."

"I'm done," said Sharpe. "I just wanted to share the experience of being attacked while doing my duty. I was set up for a fall."

"He should be sacked," muttered Cowley.

"Oh shut up," said Chalmers. "Get yourself to the toilets and get cleaned up. Somebody answer the phones. Tony, will you man the desk?"

"Yes, certainly," said Carver. "I think we should put George on the front with a big picture byline. Attacked by thugs from Vince Reay's gang when he was just trying to do his job."

"Yes, but I need words with Sharpe here," said Chalmers. "I can't have violence in the office and you can consider yourself in trouble."

"He obviously wants to sack you George," Carver told him. "And you have just given him the chance."

"You said there had been fights in the office before."

"Yes, but things were different then. Chalmers is obsessed with making cuts."

The pair were talking in the toilets, out of the way of Chalmers and his team.

"It's not a problem," said Sharpe.

Carver was aghast. "You're not taking this seriously George. You will get sacked."

"I am and I won't."

"What on earth are you thinking?"

"I'm thinking a picture tells a thousand words."

Sharpe fished inside his jacket pocket and pulled out a dog-eared photograph. He displayed it to Carver who studied it intently. The face of Gareth Chalmers beamed out of the centre of the picture in dinner jacket and tuxedo. On one side of him was Jim Jones. On the other side of him was Mrs Samantha Jones, tall and elegant in a long black chiffon dress.

"I found this amongst the pictures that Felicity gave me. I talked about it with her when I stayed the night at the mansion house. She went and asked some other questions amongst the other girls there. It turns out Mrs Jones enjoyed the green rooms herself and was often seen in the company of our dear editor. The feeling was that it all played a part in sending Mr Jones off the rails."

Carver studied the picture for a long time before saying: "I'm impressed."

"I've never blackmailed anyone before but I think I am about to," Sharpe admitted.

"Good luck."

Sharpe strode towards the door but paused as Carver unloaded one last question.

"You did sleep with her, didn't you George?"

"No comment."

TWENTY

It had been one of the longest days ever during his one year of working for The Metropolis thanks to the death of Vince Reay.

Not only had he suffered at the hands of Reay's henchmen. He had also suffered at the hands of a woman he had not even been able to talk to that day. The girlfriend of the dead hardman had phoned in to allege "doorstep harassment" of her family by Sharpe and Chalmers had called him in to his office to account for himself.

"This woman wants to know how we found out about her husband so quickly. She says it's not right that you called at the house the day after his death."

"But that's what we do," Sharpe countered. "We saw his death in the death notices and we called on his family to see what they said."

"Not anymore. Don't you know your own code of conduct Sharpe? A journalist does nothing to intrude into anybody's private life, grief or distress unless justified by overriding consideration of the public interest."

"Of course I know it. I think of it every time I am sent out on one of these knocks. It concerns me that I should be there when things are so raw, when people are coping with grief."

Chalmers nodded his agreement. The man who had unofficially allowed death knocks to make up a performance league table was now a convert to a higher cause as he tried desperately to save his own skin.

"But in this case it was probably alright," Sharpe couldn't believe he had said it. Chalmers glared at him.

"Alright to turn up on someone's doorstep within hours of his death?'

"In this case, yes. In most cases I would say no. In the case of Mrs Williamson I would say no. Where's the overriding consideration of the public interest there? It's just us wanting to get nice pictures of a child who had died tragically because it sells papers. But in the case of Vince Reay, you have a gangland execution. The public has a justified interest to know about the activities of people like him. He was gunned down on the street because of whatever he was in to. Some innocent bystanders will probably have seen it. Some innocent people might have got shot."

Sharpe felt he could talk forever. He found himself arguing in favour of the very duty he had most detested doing in his job. And Chalmers was listening. In fact he seemed subdued.

"Maybe you're right," Chalmers said. "But we need to be right every time. We need to be a bit careful about what we are doing."

"Without a doubt."

"You need to watch yourself Sharpe. This assault in the office, I have to take some action over that."

"Alright but maybe you should also consider this."

Sharpe took the photograph out of his pocket and placed it on the table. The editor's face blanched as he worked out its meaning. He had no more words. He signalled their talk was over with a wave of the hand towards the door. Sharpe picked up the photo and went back to his desk and hammered out the story of his day of distress at the hands of gangsters. He did not even look at his watch until he had finished. It was 7pm.

He signed off and made his way out of the building. He thought of joining Mary and the other reporters in The Rat but was too tired. He headed up a back lane towards his car and heard a squeal of tyres from behind him.

Sharpe looked around to see a scruffy saloon car, headlights blazing, bearing down on him. It was going straight for him. Instinctively he threw himself in to a doorway and it narrowly missed him.

Christ, it was like something out of a Raymond Chandler novel. Someone was trying to kill him. Was it Chalmers? Blackmail was a dangerous game but surely Chalmers had not had the time to stage something like this so quickly. He tried to get the registration of the car but it was too fast.

It looked like an old-style Ford Escort, not the sort of car you would imagine a gangster hitman driving. But then, whoever it was, wasn't a very good hitman.

TWENTY-ONE

Elliot, Shaun, Four, died tragically.................

When he got to the office next day, Sharpe was undecided about who to tell about the lunatic car driver. He was uninjured. It had all been over in a minute. It could just have been a drunken driver. He had too many other things to do. Besides he had not been able to get the registration number so it would be a wild goose chase. There were thousands of old cars around like the one he had seen. He suspected Chalmers might be behind it. Who knows what kind of seedy contacts a green room user might have? He couldn't go to Black. He was too weak. There were only his close friends among the reporters that he could confide in. And they were reporters. One way or another, his story would be passed on until it was all around the building. He decided that, for now, he would keep it to himself.

Tony Carver was on the desk. Cowley had telephoned in to say he was ill.

"I think he's trying to build up his compensation case," Carver laughed as he passed Sharpe a death notice he had clipped out of the paper—Shaun Elliot, four, died tragically. He was from Jarrow, a tired old riverside working town historically famous for St Bede, shipyards and unemployment.

"That might be worth looking at. You fancy it?"

"You're just as bad as the rest," Sharpe couldn't resist scoffing him. "One day in the job and you're dishing it out just the same."

"I think this one might be something," Carver said earnestly. "Besides, it's a competitive world in newspapers. If we don't go out and find the family, someone else will."

Carver dutifully took the sheet and went over to his desk. His telephone went almost as soon as he sat down. He recognised the gruff voice on the other end as Fawcett.

"George, it's not much. But this might just interest you. Your news editor friend Holmes. I sent a constable to make a few inquiries. You know they found his bike down by the staithes on the Gatehead side of the Tyne?"

"Yes, apparently he cycled in that way every day and then got all suited up at the office. I never knew that until he disappeared."

"Yes, so, of course, the first thing that comes to mind is, you know, has the chap just had enough of everything and gone and jumped in the river? A few people do."

"Yes, I know, but I was in close contact with Holmes in the days before he disappeared. He was very upbeat, a very driven type. It just doesn't ring true."

"Yes, well, that's the thing. You can never tell with this kind of business. I'm telling you this for your own information, not a story or anything, but one of my lads knocked on a few doors and spoke to an old lady who lives near the spot and who remembered seeing a chap on a bike who was being followed by a car. She says she was struck by the fact that the car driver was following him and that the cyclist might not have realised as he was on a cycleway off the road. That's all really. The only lead we have so far.'

"What sort of car was it?"

'Again very sketchy. She's a dear old lady, happy as anything to talk over a cup of tea but at the end of the day just a small car, a small, old car, possibly maroon colour."

"Oh, that's interesting. I'll bear that in mind." Fawcett had clicked his phone down before Sharpe had time to say anything else. Maybe he should have mentioned the car that was driven at him. He decided to think about it as he drove out on his job.

The register search had thrown up two Elliots in Jarrow. One address was on a private estate and the other was in an area of social housing regarded as deprived by the local council. Sharpe decided to try this address first.

He parked in a street of terraced houses. A couple of small boys were playing out when they should have been at school. His knock was answered almost immediately by a woman he guessed around the 50 mark.

"I'm sorry to bother you at a time like this. My name is George Sharpe. I'm from The Metropolis newspaper," he was becoming quite good with his polite doorstep manner, professional but caring, always softly, softly.

"That was quick," she said. "I only just put it on facebook."

Sharpe didn't know what to say. He waited.

"I'm Shaun's auntie," the woman explained. "His mum is too upset to speak, as you can imagine. But the family wants something done. That's what I've just said on facebook and here you are, the answer to a prayer."

"Anything I can do to help."

"Come here," the woman stepped out of the house, closed the door and took him by the arm. "Follow me, it's just around here."

Sharpe did what he was told. They crossed a small road and walked through an underpass to arrive at a railway line. The unmanned gate which allowed access over the line was strewn with flowers and other items of tribute to the dead boy. A photograph of the boy, obviously from a family album, had been placed on it.

"We want the railway authority crucified over this. It's always going to happen when you have a housing estate next to a railway line and they have just a gate to open and cross. Someone had left the gate open and Shaun wandered across to stroke the horses."

A tear appeared on the woman's face. She was holding together surprisingly well but shock was starting to line her face.

"What time did this happen."

"About 2pm.'

"Shouldn't Shaun have been at school?"

"He had a cold."

"But he was playing out?"

The woman started to look shifty. "Look, are you on our side or not? You don't sound like you are."

"I have to ask all kinds of questions before I write the story. We will be sympathetic and put the questions that you want answered. So Shaun was playing out was he?"

"Yes, him and another boy. They went down the line to see the horses and someone had not closed the gate properly. Shaun was just walking across when the train hit him."

"And where were his mum and dad?"

"My sister's a single mum. She was in her house with her boyfriend."

"Shaun's dad?"

"No."

Sharpe felt really sorry for little Shaun. He would have been so much better off at school. The woman was starting to look hostile again at his questioning so he changed tack.

"He's a nice looking lad," he nodded towards the picture which had been pinned on the gate." Can we get a picture like that for the paper?"

"Yes, certainly. We can go back to the house now if you like and I can find you one."

Sharpe told Mary all about the death of little Shaun in The Rat that night. She shared his sadness.

"Some kids don't get properly looked after, it's a fact," said Mary.

Sharpe nodded agreement. "The poor little bastard. His mum in bed with her latest boyfriend and him playing on a railway line. The whole culture is crap. It's not just the railway authority that is at fault here although the finger is being pointed at them."

"No," said Mary. "But they could do more couldn't they? The family does have a point. I mean an unmanned gate which can be left open, in this day and age."

"And here's the other strange thing Mary. I made a cold call intruding in to somebody's grief and I was welcomed. They were pleased I called. I just can't get my head straight about this. I think it's wrong but in this case it's right."

"There's no harm in calling at somebody's door in a professional capacity if you're polite and sensitive about it. If you're upsetting someone, just leave."

"But it is intrusion if you go there on no other information but a death notice. I mean, if you knew, through a police contact say, what had happened it is different. In this case you can say, in hindsight, that there is a huge issue to make public."

"Yes, maybe," Mary half agreed. "Can we change the subject? I am fed up with this debate. It's doing my head in."

TWENTY-TWO

For the pleasure of being deputy editor of The Metropolis, Eddie Black got to drive a nice car, a big silver Mercedes. As he drove it sensibly out of Newcastle he wondered if the perk of the car and his reasonable salary was enough to keep him in the job. It was just trouble one day after the next. The Metropolis had become a minefield which could explode at any minute with one wrong move and Chalmers had him running from one hot spot to another trying to calm things down.

Today's crisis involved Earnshaw, the reporter who had caused the paper so much trouble with his thieving and unprofessionalism. Black had been told to bring him in to face Chalmers. He had been given some support in his task. In the back of the car sat Sharpe, that odd literary kid who seemed to be coming in to his own at last as a reporter and the Irish girl, who had a lovely smile and a sexy figure but didn't seem to be a regular feature on the news lists. Her card was marked, that was for sure. But she was dead cute.

Little was said as they drove to Heaton and found the address given them by a man in the human resources department of the paper. Heaton was a lively student area, full of bright takeaways and paper trash, and the street was made up of long rows of terraced multi-occupancy.

Black rang the doorbell at no 23 and waited, hands in the trouser pockets of his blue suit. Some time elapsed without an answer. He scratched his head and turned to his two colleagues.

"When was this bloke last seen?"

"Three days ago," said Mary Rainwell. "He went to ground after he was arrested."

"Could he still be locked up?"

"No, he was given police bail straightaway," said Sharpe, "on condition that he live at this address and report to police now and again."

"So he will still be around the neighbourhood?"

"I guess so," said Sharpe. "Maybe we should spread out and knock on a few doors to see if anyone knows him."

They moved up, down and across the street making their calls. A few people answered but no one seemed to know Earnshaw.

"I know he was always away early in the morning," said one man who lived two doors away. "I never saw much of him at night. There was usually a light on around 10pm though. I think a girl had been popping in lately."

After more than an hour of knocking on doors, Black had had enough. "It's not worth it. Let's go back the office and tell Chalmers. He can maybe send him a letter or something."

The pair obediently followed him and climbed in to the Mercedes to return to the office.

Black made a call on his mobile, reporting back to Chalmers on their unsuccessful search.

A string of profanities was heard on the other side of the line. Sharpe smiled at Mary. They could hear Chalmers ranting in fury. "Don't you come back here until you have found this man, Black! I want this cleared up today. I'm going to sack him today."

Eddie Black threw his mobile in to the glove compartment of the car. "I've had enough of him, I tell you. I never know which way he is going to ask me to jump next."

"Or how high?" Sharpe tried to sound sympathetic.

"Too right. Fancy a pint? If he wants us to stay in this neck of woods I don't see why we can't enjoy some refreshments."

The trio made their way slowly along the high street. The King's Head looked warm and inviting and they made their way inside. Black went to the bar while Mary and Sharpe found seats in a corner. It was just before noon and the room was bustling. As Sharpe studied the groups of drinkers seated around the room he found himself looking at Kirsty who was seated on a high stool at the bar reading a book. He remembered she was on a day off. She spotted him and picked up her drink and headed over to join them. Sharpe saw that her book was the Lonely Planet guide to South America.

"What are you guys up to?" she asked brightly.

"Looking," said Sharpe.

"Looking for somebody," Mary tried to be more helpful.

Black rejoined them with two pints and a glass of white wine. "Oh, our number has increased. Can I get a drink for you Kirsty?"

"I'm fine thanks. Just popped in for some lunch. They do good food here."

"I didn't think you lived in Heaton," said Mary.

"I don't. I just stayed with a friend."

Kirsty appeared guarded. Mary sensed weakness and dived in.

"Which friend would that be Kirsty?"

"Well if you must know, Jeremy." Kirsty's face was becoming crimson.

"Bloody hell, Kirsty. Are you just going to sleep with every male in the newsroom or what?" Mary's voice was dagger-shaped. Sharpe put a hand on her shoulder, trying to quieten her down.

"Well there's a coincidence," said Black, who was oblivious to the tension. "We are actually looking for Jeremy. Gareth wants a word with him."

"Well that makes four of us," said Kirsty, relieved to change the subject. "I haven't seen him this morning and I don't know where he has gone.'

"You must have worn him out," said Mary. Sharpe grimaced at her to leave Kirsty alone.

"He can't be far away. He's on police bail," Black observed.

"He has to report twice a week," said Kirsty. "I know he went yesterday because he was working on his car to make sure it got him to the police station."

"His car. What sort of car would that be?'' asked Sharpe.

"I don't know the make. I'm a journalist not a petrol-head," said Kirsty. "It was just an old hatchback that some uncle of his was scrapping. So he got it passed on to him and he reckoned he had been working on it ever since.'

"You do know him well Kirsty," said Mary.

"I like him actually although I seem to be the only person in the world who does."

"What do you like about him for God's sake?" Mary asked.

"Well his aggression. I like men who are aggressive," Kirsty was not a girl for keeping secrets.

"This guy is so aggressive he has started doing naughty things," Sharpe said. "You should be careful Kirsty. He's also a bible-wielding freak isn't he?"

"Not that I know of," said Kirsty. "The bible's the last thing I would connect with him. He's a bad boy." Sharpe thought he saw a glint of mischief in her eye.

"Where does that leave us with finding him?" Black asked.

"We are looking for a bible-wielding lunatic in an old car who keeps popping up in bizarre situations," Sharpe told him. "Don't suppose you have any idea about the registration mark of the car do you Kirsty?"

"Nope, not a clue and I don't like the insinuation that I am in a friendship with a lunatic."

"Oh Kirsty, be honest. It's just anyone with zippered trousers for you isn't it? Be honest."

Sharpe eyeballed Mary again. "You're not helping Mary. Just leave her be."

Mary tutted and looked away her chin lifting defiantly. Kirsty was still trying to defend her choice of boyfriend.

"A lunatic wouldn't have a degree in psychology, would he?" she asked defiantly.

"Guess not," Sharpe admitted. "Where did he fit that in, the University of God?"

"No, the Open University. What he was really interested in was hypnosis."

"Daresay he put you under a few times," Mary couldn't help herself. Sharpe threw up his arms in exasperation at her.

"No, I'm much too flighty anyway," Kirsty admitted. "I told him there was no way he was putting a spell on me."

"Right, I say we split up," said Sharpe. "Eddie, perhaps you and Kirsty can stay around here and wait for Earnshaw to turn up. He has to sometime. Mary and I will go and see Mrs Holmes. I think she has to know what is going on."

Black nodded his agreement, happy to be left in the pub with Kirsty. He had started browsing through her travel guide. Mary frowned but followed Sharpe's lead.

"Are you thinking what I am thinking?" he demanded, once they were outside in the street.

"What?" Mary was nonplussed.

"It's Earnshaw. He is the key to all this. The old car is the clue. I am pretty sure he tried to kill me the other night in a dirty old hatchback. He has done something to Holmes. And I hope it's just a kidnapping."

Mary's mouth sagged open. "God, I never thought."

"Yes, you were too busy moralising. Do you have any women friends at all?"

"Yes, I do."

"Where are they?"

"Back home in Ireland."

"You need to start making some here to counter balance all the enemies you're making for yourself."

Mary was nearly lost for words. "I'll think about it," she said

TWENTY-THREE

S ue Holmes bore the tired face of a woman who couldn't sleep and had to
continue looking after her two young children as if everything was normal.
She seemed to perk slightly on opening her front door and seeing Sharpe there
with Mary. Sharpe guessed she was hoping for some good news. He was not
sure he had any. He was operating on gut instinct.

They were invited in and she disappeared in to her kitchen emerging with
some snacks and a bottle of wine which she placed on a coffee table in the
middle of her living room.

"Mary and I have been talking about your husband, Sue, and we have
a theory. We think his disappearance has something to do with one of the
reporters, a lad called Jeremy Earnshaw.

"I know that name only too well. Phil was always ranting off about
Earnshaw and his dirty tricks. He hated him. Said he was the sort of reporter
who gave the rest a bad image."

Mary chipped in. "I don't think anyone would disagree with you there. He's
the most obnoxious person that I have ever met."

"I think Earnshaw has had some sort of breakdown," said Sharpe, "and is
capable of doing a lot of harm. I think he tried to knock me over in a car the
other night."

Sharpe suddenly felt guilty about suspecting Chalmers. It was just as well
he had kept the whole thing to himself until now.

136

"Oh really," Sue's face was white with horror. "So what are you going to do?"

"We are trying to find Earnshaw. If we can find him we can maybe find Phil. It's just a hunch. I don't want to raise your hopes."

"But you will have to contact the police. Surely, they will launch a search for him?"

"We don't have time to persuade the police to act on my theory. As far as they are concerned, Phil is a missing person, a possible suicide or freak accident by a river. Somehow or other we have to find him ourselves. If we can't find him we have to find Earnshaw."

Mary was suddenly inspired. "Iphones. I know how to track iphones. All I need is the number of the phone. We've all got iphones haven't we?"

Sharpe was sceptical. "Yes, but don't you need a special app and ID numbers and all that to track a mobile? How can we possibly do all that?"

"No," Mary was positive. "I just need the phone number. I've got the phone tracker spy gadget on my iphone."

"Phone tracker spy gadget! So that's it! That's how you knew I was with Felicity in the mansion house isn't it? You're a bloody stalker. You said it was Geoff. Mary, you are becoming devious!"

"Dear God, you have to be just a little devious in this game George Sharpe. It's time you stopped being so shiny and pure. You were up to something that night weren't you?"

"Up to something. I'm single. I have no one to answer to. And yet I am under electronic surveillance. And that's rich about me being too shiny and pure, coming from a catholic girl," Sharpe was wagging his head, unable to look her in the eye.

"Can you two stop bickering and get back to finding my husband please?" Sue's voice was shaky as she pleaded with them. I don't think we have much time."

"Hell, yes, where do we start?" Sharpe was suddenly back on track. "Earnshaw will probably have a company mobile won't he?"

"Sort of," Sue chipped in. "He had bought himself an iphone and got the company to refund him the cash. Phil was always on about that because he couldn't get one for himself. Had to use mine sometimes when he was somewhere away from work."

"Did he borrow it on the day that he went missing?" asked Sharpe.

"No. There was a fault on it so we couldn't use it. He said he would take it in for repair.'

"Oh, let's have the number," said Sharpe. "We can try to trace it."

"I don't have a clue," said Sue. "I never remember phone numbers."

"Get it off your landline," said Mary. "It's bound to be on there somewhere."

Sue did as she was told and Mary punched the number in to her iphone.

"It's giving me a location" she announced triumphantly. "It's down by the docks."

"Let's go said Sharpe. The guy has been missing for three days. He could be near death."

TWENTY-FOUR

The trace led them to a small riverside industrial estate on the outskirts of Newcastle. They motored through the estate following the signal until they could drive no further. They were outside a wire fenced compound in total darkness. Sharpe positioned the car so that its main beams picked out the entrance gate to the compound.

"I didn't spy on your phone the other night George, honest. It was Geoff who gave you away," Mary's voice was deadly earnest.

"Alright, I'm sorry. I think I'm getting a bit jumpy. I'm losing track of who I can trust and who I can't."

"Me too. I'm down to four fingers, I think."

"Yes, you, me, Carver and maybe Holmes."

"So, what's this place?" Mary was staring at the entrance gate signs.

"It's a storage depot," Sharpe said. "There are hundreds of big containers in there, the sort they use on ships. Don't say he has been dumped in one of them."

"Must be," said Mary. "What do we do?"

"Call the police I suppose. But hang on a minute."

His ears had picked up the sound of an approaching car. He reversed his car in to a parking space off the street and switched off engine and lights. In the dark they could make out the shape of a hatchback car approaching.

"I bet that's a maroon hatchback that hasn't been washed in weeks," said Sharpe.

"It's Earnshaw alright," gasped Mary, looking at him with just a hint of fear in her eyes. "Look, I just put his number in to my spy gadget and he's only a couple of streets away."

"There's two of us Mary, only one of him," he reassured her.

"That's what I like about you. No messing around with polite gentilities like "after you" or "leave this to me". You might as well just say: I'm just one of the boys."

"Shush for a minute," he commanded and they watched as Earnshaw emerged from the car, a thin figure wearing a hoodie and jeans, looking like a car thief. He used a key to open the gates and drove through.

"Twenty-four hour storage facility and Earnshaw is visiting. Holmes could be alive," he said.

"Let's get him out," said Mary.

Sharpe turned the ignition key and eased the car forward. He rammed his foot down as Earnshaw turned to investigate and braked so that the car was parked between the gates blocking any means of exit.

Mary was out of the car before him and ran straight for Earnshaw who stared at her in astonishment. She swung a fist and blood spurted from his face. Sharpe caught up to her and saw that her phone was clenched inside her fist. She started gently prizing her fingers from it.

"That's a Belfast trick," she explained.

Sharpe grabbed Earnshaw by his hoodie and rammed his arm up behind his back. Earnshaw was using his other hand to try and stem the flow of blood from his face.

"Take us to him Jeremy," he said coolly. "It's all over for you now."

Earnshaw half walked and half stumbled for what seemed an age. The distance involved was only fifty metres. They walked along in semi-darkness between a row of storage containers until he finally stopped at one. Its steel doors were fortified by huge iron lever bars held in a padlock.

Sharpe released the whimpering Earnshaw from his grip. "You open it now Jeremy and no tricks or it will be me throwing the punches as well as Mary."

Earnshaw did as he was told unlocking the padlock and then using all his strength to pull back one of the locking bars and then the other. He was finally able to open one of the doors.

Holmes was a sorry sight. He was wearing an arctic parka and pants and walking boots. Earnshaw had wrapped him up well in winter sports gear to leave him bound and gagged on a wooden chair. The hood around his face meant that Sharpe could not see his eyes and the lack of response from Holmes worried him. He saw a torch lying by the chair and picked it up. He shone it in Holmes's face and his body jerked into life.

"Thank God for that," said Sharpe before rounding on Earnshaw who was by now in tears. "What were you thinking of Jeremy? You could have killed him."

"I just wanted to be top of the league," Earnshaw mumbled. "He wouldn't let me."

Mary was on her mobile to the police and still nursing her hand as she made the call.

They took Holmes immediately to the nearest, warmest place—Mary's flat. Her roommate Emma was at home and watched the drama in total astonishment, unable to move from the sofa in case she missed anything.

Sitting in front of a portable electric fire, Holmes told them of his ordeal, talking non-stop for an hour.

"He left me in a dark, cold place for hours on end, the bastard. He eased his conscience by visiting every three or four hours with water and food, day and night. And always the bible passages. The Corinthians, Genesis, Romans. He had a big thing about Genesis. He read these passages over so many times I can't get them out of my head.

Holmes started reciting as if to get it out of his system: "In the beginning God created the heavens and the earth. The earth was formless and void, and darkness was over the surface of the deep, and the Spirit of God was moving over the surface of the waters . . . .

" By the seventh day God completed His work which He had done, and He rested on the seventh day from all His work which He had done. Then God blessed the seventh day and sanctified it, because in it He rested from all His work which God had created and made."

On and on it went until Holmes finally ran out of words. Sharpe looked at Mary: "We have to get him back to what he was. He's been brainwashed."

"Yeah, in a dark room with that idiot babbling away in your ear. It's enough to turn anyone."

"I think that was the intention. I think Earnshaw was seriously trying to programme him in some sort of way. I suppose it just shows how mad he is."

"Yes," Mary agreed. "Best thing now is that he gets his head around something else."

"Too right. Look Phil," Sharpe was almost shouting at his boss. "You are needed. We have to move fast. We have to tell management that we are out of the building. It can't go on."

Holmes blinked and a glimmer of his old self returned to his face. "Yes, I can't be bullied anymore."

It was almost 6am. Time had seemed irrelevant for hours but now they headed for the car and explained to Holmes all that had been happening. By the time they got to the office he seemed his old self again.

He wandered around the newsroom shaking hands with the early birds and telling them about his experience.

When he got to the newsdesk, there was no Cowley. Tony Carver looked very much in charge and sitting next to him was Mary, who had quickly made up in the toilets and taken Cowley's seat.

"How the hell did she get that job? She was bottom of the list every day." Holmes was staring at Sharpe. Sharpe shrugged his shoulders. Neither Holmes nor Mary would ever know the truth. "I think Chalmers was trying to look good by promoting females," he said.

Their conversation was interrupted by Chalmers who had arrived at an unusually early hour, a sure sign he was up to something. "Oh, you're alive," he said to Holmes without much enthusiasm. He made for his office but Holmes stepped in his way.

"Thanks for your interest," he said. "Now, tell me what you are going to do about the fact that I have been kidnapped, held captive for three days, and almost killed by hypothermia? I would have thought I should be your main story today."

Carver piped up from his seat at the news desk. "I should think so. We should let this story run. I've just had a check made with the police and Earnshaw is in a cell. We can expect charges shortly."

Chalmers flushed crimson. He shouted for his chief sub Smithson to join him. "This is in-house," he moaned. "We can't make big fuss about it. We will look fools. What will higher management say? Isn't that right Smithson?"

Smithson gave a brief nod but looked very uncomfortable as if he wanted to be a distance away from this confrontation.

"That's it," said Holmes. "We are out. You can't do anything you like Chalmers, not anymore. You can find us in The Rat if you have anything meaningful to tell us."

Holmes started walking. Smithson spoke up: "C'mon Phil. We all have mortgages to pay. We can't afford to strike. The subs won't come out. You will be on your own."

Holmes ignored him and continued walking towards the exit. He was followed by Sharpe and Mary and Tony Carver. Other reporters started to follow. The subs stayed where they were. Two photographers who made up the early shift for pictures looked on with bemused faces.

Kirsty walked out followed by Eddie Black.

TWENTY-FIVE

Chalmers was in the executive dining room of Metro Edifice glumly looking at a first edition of The Metropolis. The front page was devoted to a weak story about possible signings and transfers for the team and its standing in the premiership, which was middle of the table unexciting. Complementing it as a single column was a health story about the dangers of sunbathing if there was a good summer. Some chance in the North East of England. There was no crime, no scandal, no nasties to spice the page up.

He picked at his fish and chips. It had been three days now since those shit reporter hacks went out on strike and, he had to admit, their presence was being missed. Chalmers had never realised just how difficult it was to replace good hard news reporters with on the patch experience. He had tried hiring some young kids but they were useless. Anyone could write a news story but it took an operator to come up with the goods time after time in all kinds of situations.

His thoughts were interrupted by the blunt Yorkshire voice of Owen Michaelson.

"You had your chance Chalmers. I told you that Morton was on your case. I warned you that you had to do something and you did nothing. It's out of your hands now."

The colour drained fom Chalmers' face. Michaelson seemed to tower over him.

"You never sorted this mess out with Earnshaw. Now you've got a bloody strike on your hands and circulation is dropping like a stone. I don't like coming up to Newcastle all the time Chalmers so this time I am going to make sure I don't have to come back. You're finished."

"But I was told to make cuts," Chalmers pleaded. "There wouldn't be a strike if I didn't have to make cuts."

"You did it all the wrong way, trying to get rid of half the reporters and what a scandalous way to do it. This bloody League of Death. I warned you about that. Your number two has told me all about this horrible business, how you turned a blind eye and then tried to destroy all evidence of your involvement. It's shameful. This chap Cowley is going as well. He's the one who started it. You'll get payoffs if you behave yourself and get out the door quick."

"Black told you about it?"

"Yes, he did the honourable thing and got it off his chest. He has resigned and is heading down to London. I am putting a word in for him with a colleague of mine down there. He should do alright."

"So what's happening in Newcastle?" Chalmers shoved his uneaten food to one side. He wanted a drink.

Michaelson puffed out his chest. "I've been talking to Olwen Hardy. The Metropolis is to get a female editor. We want a new direction and we have already found the right woman. She is from outside the North East, a new broom.

"Holmes will be her deputy and we will get a new news editor. Tony Carver is an experienced hand and will look after the desk until that appointment is made. Olwen reckons we should have a female presence on the news desk as well. Girl called Mary Rainwell."

"Olwen? she's never here. Rainwell? I have already promoted her," Chalmers was shaking slightly as he remembered the photo that Sharpe had flashed at him on two occasions now, the second to win his friend's promotion.

"Olwen will be here regularly from now. We want the paper back to its usual self, with a smile on its face. We want reporters at full strength, may even appoint a couple more. Job cuts will be made at higher level starting with you and Cowley and Black. More troops, less generals."

Chalmers knew there was no way back for him. "Can I get stuff out of my office," he asked quietly. "I need a drink."

"Eddie the security man is waiting to take you to your office and get your things. He will then escort you out of the building and you will not be able to return."

"Can I say goodbye to the staff?"

"Are you sure you want to?" Michaelson demanded. "I am told you're not very popular."

"Being an editor is not a popularity contest," said Chalmers. "I have been here from the start and I want to say goodbye to the staff."

TWENTY-SIX

It wasn't a wind of change blowing through The Metropolis. It was a tornado. The victorious reporters had marched back in with a promise of pay increases and job security. Black had walked out with them but did not return. Before heading down the M1 he had spoken enthusiastically in The Rat about his plans to follow the Inca Trail in Peru. Holmes had been given garden leave to recover from his ordeal and prepare to be the new deputy editor. Earnshaw had been interviewed by a Home Office psychologist while in jail and diagnosed schizoid. Police found a number of text books on hypnosis in his flat. Marker pen lines showed he had been particularly studying mind control and other brainwashing techniques. Earnshaw was looking more sinister by the minute. The psychologist concluded that imprisoning Holmes inside a metal container for hours on end had been the destabilising and disorienting prelude to a programme of brainwashing that would have followed. Earnshaw's plan was to make Holmes in to a Manchurian Candidate puppet who would follow his orders and provide a path back for him to his job.

Chalmers was uprooted and cast aside like a diseased tree. Yet Sharpe had to admire the way he still managed to look pompously important even as he gave an impromptu farewell speech in the main office to all his staff.

"As you know, London wants big changes and they start at the top with me. I am not going graciously. I consider my departure from a job I love as something that has been forced on me by people that I trusted. Through no fault of mine, a rotten apple got in to the barrel and the management view is that the whole barrel, more or less, has to go."

Chalmers paused and stared across the room at the vacant office of Eddie Brown before going on. "I am now going to enjoy the beauty of my garden, something I have not been able to do for years, while I contemplate my next move. I don't expect to be out of the game for long.

"I hope we have all learned a lesson from the mess that has been created here by one or two individuals overstepping the line. One of these individuals, I understand, was yesterday sentenced to two years in jail for theft, burglary and kidnap. We have indeed had a psychopath in our ranks without realising it until it was too late."

Sharpe noticed Holmes wagging his head in disapproval. He didn't have to guess what he was thinking. It was the duplicitous man management of Chalmers that had allowed Earnshaw to survive in the job as his crimes escalated from simple theft to kidnap and threats to kill.

"An editor is only as good as his staff and it's sad to say that one or two of my staff have let me down. That's not to say that I have not made mistakes myself. One of them was to underestimate the importance of those of us who go out on the front line every day."

Sharpe noticed a quizzical look on the face of Smithson, the veteran sub who had pleaded for the reporters not to walk out.

"I am talking about the general news reporters who operate out on the doorsteps of this fine city and bring in the stories that sell our paper. I can't speak too highly of them. Just how valuable they are came home to me when I read The Metropolis after their strike started. I took them for granted and for that I am sorry."

This was amazing. Here was a cynical, amoral and ruthless man speaking the truth and nothing but the truth for once in his life. The reporters had never dared to think they could be that important. Their action had been a desperate one but now it was vindicated. They were the front line and what good was an army without a front line? And yet they didn't even realise their strength.

"I don't want to say much more other than to thank my staff as a whole for their wonderful support during my tenure. I shall miss all of you."

Chalmers' voice was tailing off and Sharpe looked round the newsroom to see the reason for it. The newspaper's new editor had arrived complete with her laptop and iPad. She was young, freshfaced and cut an attractive figure in white blouse shirt, dark pinstripe trousers and long zipped boots.

Chalmers looked to Michaelson who had been standing alongside him, his face wrapped in resignation. Michaelson nodded to him to continue.

Chalmers' voice became a croak. "It seems I now have the pleasure of introducing you all to my replacement. Meet your new editor, Ms Fiona Pilkington-Smith."

Pilkington-Smith smiled graciously and eased her way across to centre stage between Chalmers and Michaelson.

"Alright, well you may as well have a two for one in speeches today," she said cheerily.

"I would ask all staff for their support as I move in to this job to give a new direction and a new style to a very marketable product.

"There has been too much going on off the ball here. We need to concentrate on the ball and keep it moving forward. How we will do that?"

She threw back her long red hair and smiled seductively.

"By competing to win the ball. By that I mean an aggressive but fair approach to the compilation of a first class news service. Our general news reporters are our strikers and I won't have them hindered in any way.

"Of course a lot has been said in recent weeks about the tactics of our reporters, the foot-in-the-door style, the harassment of people who should be left alone while in grief. It's right that you can't have journalists going in to people's houses and taking things without their permission.

"Journalists are subject to the law just as much as anyone else and have to work within its confines."

Then her eyes seemed to fire up as she slowly looked around the room making sure she took everyone in.

"But we will continue to operate on the doorstep just as before. There was nothing wrong with the system until one or two individuals went too far.

"We have noted the comments about intrusion in to the private grief of families and will take them on board. There will be no league tables for death knocks although I still think some kind of performance related measures might be appropriate.

"I myself will be pushing for more reporters as I believe we can provide extra pages of news for our readers and I will be expecting them all to be out there knocking on doors fighting their corner for the paper. If we don't get there first then the Sentinel or some tv person will. I will be holding a personal one-to-one interview with every reporter we have over the next few days to discuss this."

She was confident and sassy, a natural for the job. She took some questions and Sharpe asked one. "Does that mean death knocks go on as before. We cold call all the unusual death notices."

The half smile vanished from her lips. Her eyes became cold slits. "Maybe cold call is not the right choice of words. But make no mistake, we have to do this and, unless there is a law passed that says we can't, we will."

"The code of conduct, is that not going to be taken on board?"

"Of course, but we can't judge the situation until we get out there and establish the facts of it. We must collect our news aggressively."

It was more of the same. The Metropolis had a new woman editor, a new deputy editor, a new news desk and it was basically being told to carry on in the same old way, in pursuit of death and tragedy.

After listening to her, Sharpe rang Geoff on his mobile.

"You know that South America trip you wanted to do?"

"Oh yes. I can't wait."

"Well I'm up for it. I'm putting my notice in today."

"Good for you. By the way I spoke to my publisher and he's interested in a book about the mansion house."

"Good. I'll write it while we are on the road."

Sharpe looked across at Mary Rainwell, the new Metropolis deputy news editor, She had a gleam in her eye and had been nodding her head in agreement with everything her new editor said.

He wondered how he would tell her about his decision.

It would have to wait. He would enjoy a pint in The Rat before putting in his notice and then telling his workmates about what he was doing.

It was a clear day outside and he took a deep breath of fresh air. The city was early morning busy, people rushing everywhere. As he strolled on he noticed Felicity walking towards him. She was different, not all glammed up. She wore hardly any makeup at all.

"Where are you going?" he demanded.

"Hello George. What a surprise. Guess what? I've got an interview with this new editor of yours. She's looking for more reporters.'

"I thought you were still at college."

"I'm in my last year and she said I may be able to come in and get some work experience with a view to getting a job as a reporter."

"Work for nothing for a bit?"

"Yes, but not forever. I'll get something out of it and then move on down to London."

"Good for you."

Not only did Felicity look different, she sounded different. Her voice was less sexy, more serious.

"You know George, I owe you a big thank-you."

"Oh yes, what for?"

"You made me see how silly I have been."

"I don't think you are silly Felicity and I have certainly never said that to you. I don't judge people. You are what you are and I find you likeable for it."

"Yes, but the sex industry is not where I need to be. And I've given it up thanks to you. When you didn't sleep with me that night I was a bit put out at first. But I knew you liked me and it made me think. You actually treated me the way a girl should be treated and it was nice. I want more of that so I have changed, turned my back on sleeping with strangers for extra income."

"Oh well, good for you. I would hate to think of my sisters doing that sort of thing."

"I know."

"Good luck in your interview with Pilkington-Smith. She looks like a very attractive slave driver."

They parted company but Sharpe shouted after her. "I would try to make Mary your first friend up there. You need her to keep her mouth shut about you."

Felicity smiled. "I know."

"Tell her I'm in the pub will you and I've got something I need to tell her."

"Okay. You're fond of her aren't you?"

"Yes, unfortunately."

He wandered on. He felt as though a weight was lifting off his shoulders. He needed beer. He maybe needed several beers.

Printed in Great Britain
by Amazon.co.uk, Ltd.,
Marston Gate.